The Goddess's Wards

Danielle Paquette-Harvey

1984 –

Cover by Danielle Paquette-Harvey

ISBN (paperback) 978-1-7388313-5-7

First Edition: April 2023

Published by: Danielle Paquette-Harvey

http://daniellephauthor.com

https://www.instagram.com/daniellephauthor

Subscribe to my mailing list so you don't miss anything!

daniellephauthor.com

Follow me
- Facebook: Danielle Paquette-Harvey
- Instagram: daniellephauthor

Other books by the author
All my books are available on Amazon.

Prequel to the Longing mates series
- The prophecy - ISBN 978-1777572105

Longing mates Series
A powerful, alluring vampire prince. The strong daughter of the Alpha. Born enemies, tied by an unbreakable bond. Multiple times Best Seller in different countries. Read the series that started it all.

1. Age-Old Enemies - ISBN 978-1777572136

2. A Beloved Sin - ISBN 978-1777572150

3.   The Fallen - ISBN 978-1-7782178-5-2

ISBN 978-1-7782178-5-2

Blood and Kisses Series
1.   **Cursed King – coming soon**

Half-angel's daughter Series
1.   **Devoured by Darkness – coming soon**

Charity books

- A Wicked Taste of Fate – An Anthology - ISBN 978-1-7782178-6-9

  Please note: This dark fantasy anthology book contains eight short stories from different authors. All the profits go to Ste-Justine's, a children's hospital in Montreal.

Danielle Paquette-Harvey

The Goddess's Wards

Contents

Moon Elve's Lands
Soul Nymph's Domain
St-Lawrence River
David's Pack
Sleeping Lake
Eurynomos Sepuclher
Hemera's S

Nymph
ed Grove
Valley of Nysa
Vampire's Castle
Human Town

Preface

The Forgotten History

The ancient texts spoke of the end of a dark age and the dawn of a new era of peace and prosperity. All celebrated the day the demon was locked away by the Moon Goddess. But the ancient texts don't relate everything, for history has forgotten that a price had to be paid to bring this peace.

This book will reveal what happened centuries before "A Beloved Sin."

Discover the truth about the people who were called the Goddess's Wards.

Prologue (Unknown)

A Cursed Gift

The moon was full, and light snowflakes were falling from the sky. The cold wind blew on my skin, making me shiver. Our ancestors had foretold that a bright light would shine, ending a dark age of blood and death. Everyone in town gathered quickly when the light tore through the darkness of the night. We followed it right into the dead of the wood. In front of us stood a woman. Her hair was blonde, almost white, undulating in waves, going way down her back. She wore a long white dress. The air seemed to glow with the light of her golden crown.

Further back, I could see her silver chariot pulled by two snow-white winged horses. A powerful aura emanated from her, and I could only hope the prophecies were accurate: that she was the one who would end the reign of terror of the murderous demon, Eurynomos.

She stood in silence, observing us. I stiffened, and my heart raced when she gestured toward me.

"You! Step forward."

I held back my breath as everyone turned my way, staring at me. People moved to the side, making a path between the woman and me. I swallowed hard and walked toward her. I was scared as hell and didn't know what to expect.

She looked at me kindly as I approached her, and I immediately relaxed. When I got in front of her, I asked timidly,

"Are you the one the prophecy stated? Are you the one who will rid us of Eurynomos?"

The woman nodded.

"I am, though it's not as simple as ridding you of Eurynomos."

"What do you mean?"

"Eurynomos cannot simply be killed. He is a powerful demon. But I have sealed him in a sepulcher, protected by a powerful spell."

A gasp was heard at those words, and whispers were heard. Before I could say anything more, a howl tore through the night. I stepped back, screaming, as a giant gray wolf appeared between the woman and me, growling menacingly at me. Looking around the woods, I realized dozens of wolves were surrounding us. People pressed against each other as the wolves came closer.

The woman put her hand on the giant wolf's head, and he stopped growling.

She spoke to the wolf, "Calm down. They mean me no harm."

The wolf nodded and bowed his head. I couldn't believe my eyes as his body started to shift right in front of me. His paws and bones elongated into arms, legs, and spine. It all happened quickly; before I knew it, a full-grown naked man was kneeling before the woman. I was too surprised to be scared. My mouth went agape when I realized that all the wolves had also shifted to humans. People started to stir from this, and some tried to get away, but the woman sent a wave of magic, stopping them in their way.

She spoke with authority and kindness, "Stay calm. There is nothing to fear."

People seemed to relax at her words. She added, "Humans! These are wolf shifters. You might not have heard of them, but they have lived among you for centuries."

Her words resonated in my mind. I had never heard of wolf shifters. An old woman asked, "Are they the werewolves that devour my sheep at night?"

The man to my side scoffed at those words. The woman answered, "What you might have heard or believed about wolf shifters is probably wrong and exaggerated."

I pondered for a while. Werewolves. They were only legends, or so I thought. Never could I have believed that they existed. Yet, I was now surrounded by werewolves. It was scary yet exciting.

The kneeling man spoke deeply, not daring to lift his head toward the woman, "My Goddess."

My eyes widened as I repeated, "Goddess?"

The woman nodded and gestured to the man.

"You may rise." Then she looked at the people from my town and me. "Humans! Fear not, for I am the Moon Goddess."

People gasped at her words. It certainly explained the aura of power I felt surrounding her and how her words could instantly calm people. This night challenged everything that I ever believed was true. Murmurs arose from the crowd. I remembered reading the legends of the Moon Goddess once in an old folklore book, but otherwise, I had never heard of her. My heart was racing, and I should have been scared, but somehow I felt excited and ready to accept this new knowledge.

She continued, "As I said, I have sealed the demon, Eurynomos. I have chosen all of you to be the guardians of his sepulcher."

Questions started to arise from the crowd.

"Chose us? How?"

"Why us?"

"Do we need to fight a demon?"

The wolf-shifters were silent, waiting for the Moon Goddess to keep talking. I couldn't help but appreciate their respect for her compared to my people.

She smiled when a kid asked, "How are we supposed to do this?"

She spoke in a firm voice, "Humans! I will give you the gift of magic. You will be able to wield the elements, brew powerful potions, or call on mystical forces. This is my gift to you for becoming guardians of the demon."

She turned towards the wolf shifters. My gaze shifted from the Goddess to the man standing beside me. His green eyes caught my eyes, and I lost myself in them momentarily, gazing upon his deepest secrets. His black hair was messy, and he had light stubble. He smirked as my eyes fell onto his muscled chest. He was handsome, and I caught myself wondering if he was single. I scolded myself, now was not the time to think about finding a boyfriend.

The man turned his head towards the Goddess when she spoke.

"Werewolves, I will gift you a fated mate. You will find, only once in your lifetime, a twin soul. Someone made especially for you, as you will also be made for them. An attraction so strong it's impossible to resist. A never-ending love and a more powerful bond than anything you thought existed. Giving you the power to sense what your mate is feeling and speak through their mind as your bond increases, making you one with this person. You shall take care of your fated mate and overcome challenges together."

As she spoke those words, something clicked through me, and the man's eyes flickered. He looked at me, his eyes heavy with desire. My heart pounded in my chest. I wanted to go to him; I needed to be with him. Sure, he was handsome, but at this moment, I felt like I had known him forever. I wanted to be in his arms, never to go away. Was this the bond she was talking about? If it was, it was undoubtedly the most powerful thing I had ever felt, and I didn't want to fight it.

The Moon Goddess smiled, looking at the man and me before pointing at us.

"These two will be your new leaders. Your two races must associate together, as you are all my wards. Learn from one another. Master your powers. Always be prepared in case the demon should be freed. Many perils will await you."

My mate told the Goddess, "I, Alpha Cyrus of the dark forest pack, accept your gift with humility. We will happily welcome the humans in our pack."

I frowned. "Wait, what? A pack? Alpha?"

The Moon Goddess smiled. "You have a lot to learn. And you must understand that the werewolves' way of leading a pack, or the human way of living in society, will not work. You will now form a new kind of society, a new form of pack. A pack of werewolves-witches. Live in harmony with the forest, and build a strong society with rules that please both werewolves and witches."

The man stared into my eyes deeply, and I could stare at his soul. He was strong, had a kind heart, and wished to protect his loved ones. We had so much to discover, and I was eager to learn everything about him. He nodded, not breaking eye contact with me.

"Understood," he answered the Goddess before adding to me, "I can't wait to get to know you better."

Heat rose to my cheeks, and my heart fluttered at those words. I answered back, "I can't wait either."

The werewolves began to mix with the people from my town, trying to get to know them. People in the crowd started looking at each other, exchanging words. Some people were amazed to see that they could summon elements and magic.

The Goddess said, "You shall create a new pack here, close to Eurynomos's sepulcher."

The man grabbed my hand, and I swear I felt a surge of magic traveling through me as he did, sending sparks through my spine. My heart was racing in my chest. I looked at the Goddess, "Thank you for those wonderful gifts."

She shook her head. "You should hear me out before thanking me. As I am afraid that those gifts come with a curse."

Everyone stopped talking and stared at her at those words. What curse? She hadn't spoken about any curses. Frightened, we hung on to the Goddess's words as she told us of the horrible curse that now bound us to the protection of the demon's sepulcher.

Chapter 1 (Matthew)

Born with an expiration date

*** Centuries later ***

I woke up to the scent of coffee and eggs. I wasn't in a hurry to get up. My head throbbed from the lack of sleep. I was still sore from yesterday's race. I loved participating in those, even though I didn't have to. As the Alpha's son, I was faster than most wolves of the pack. But the race was different every time.

Since our pack consisted of witches and werewolves, we changed the race so that everyone could have a chance to win. Last night's race was prepared so that witches had a better chance of winning than werewolves. I was proud when I managed to finish second. Those born with the gift of magic and a wolf had a real advantage, but there were very few of them. Those born without magic or a wolf were usually in charge of preparing the race, as they couldn't compete with us. But we still organized races made especially for them. They were essential members of the pack, and we didn't want them to feel left out.

The feast following the race was a celebration in which everyone partakes. Yesterday's was one of the best I've seen. We celebrated for hours, and I remember dancing with Kelly all night, her blonde hair swaying to the rhythm of the music. She was one of my best friends. Although we once had a small affair, we agreed to stay just friends. But we both knew that on nights of celebration, after drinking, things tended to heat up between us. It was something I was looking for as much as she did. As long as we were both single and willing, it was a game she liked to play with me.

The smell of food got the better of me. I put on a pair of jeans and a black t-shirt, then shaved before combing my brown hair. When I decided I looked good enough, I got to the kitchen.

"Happy birthday, Mat!" joyfully shouted my dad, Esme, my brother Bryan, and Kelly.

Esme was the oldest witch of the pack. At ninety-two years old, I knew she had little time to go. But she was like a mother to me. Esme helped my father raise me, as my mother died giving birth to me. Kelly, Bryan, and my dad hugged me while Esme watched, smiling.

I was glad to see them but wasn't happy that it was my birthday. Today was a gloomy day for me. I dreaded this moment all my life. Twenty-six years ago, I was born on a blessed night. I was the most precious member of the pack. I was the one chosen, born with the mark. I was to be cherished until the day I would be sacrificed. This year was the last that I would live. No one ever made it older than twenty-six years old. Sometime before my twenty-seventh birthday, the demon's seal would weaken. When that happens, my blood will be spilled, and I will die so Eurynomos doesn't escape his sepulcher. I never understood why they called this a "blessed night." I was born with an expiration date.

That's why my brother Bryan was the next in line to become the next Alpha, even though I was the oldest. Everyone in the pack knew I would never be the Alpha, but they still paid me respect while I was alive.

"Sherry didn't come to see me?" I asked.

My dad shook his head.

"She's busy with her youngest pup. She'll probably be there later today."

Sherry was Bryan's mother. She and my dad dated a few years ago. But she didn't want to become the pack's Luna. Too many responsibilities. So they split up but stayed friends. Still, she looked after me like I was her son.

After breakfast, I exited the pack house with Kelly. It was a sunny summer day, and the sun's rays felt hot on my skin. We walked toward the forest. We had to stop whenever we crossed someone's path as they wanted to wish me a happy birthday. They didn't know it was my birthday because I was the Alpha's son. They knew it because I was the one to be killed. With each generation, it became increasingly difficult to sacrifice the "treasured member" of the pack, as they called him, the emotional weight taking its toll on people.

We had a big wall surrounding our pack's houses. The name of everyone who had been sacrificed over the years was written on it. It all started when we received this curse from the Goddess, and people were tired of it. I felt sick, knowing that soon my name would be added to the wall.

"Be safe!" Charles shouted as we crossed the dreaded wall and ventured into the forest. Charles was one of the best guards in the pack.

I gestured to him. "Sure!"

He nodded, his red hair swaying in the wind, then added eagerly, grinning, "Oh! I almost forgot! Happy birthday!"

I smiled at him. "Thanks!"

I breathed a sigh of relief as we headed deeper into the woods. Kelly laughed, her crystal clear voice echoing around me.

"You're getting a lot of attention today!"

"Too much!" I replied, annoyed.

Kelly looked at me with her deep chocolate eyes. We stepped over a small stream.

"You can't blame them for wishing you a happy birthday."

I knew she was right, but still…

"It's a constant reminder that this is my last birthday."

She walked in silence for a while, staring at the ground. She spoke; her voice was barely audible.

"I know. You're my best friend, Matthew. I…"

She stopped talking, her voice broken, a pained expression on her face. She gasped in surprise and stared at me when I grasped her hand, pulling her into an embrace. She relaxed into my arms, and her breath felt hot on my neck. I knew she dreaded the day I would need to be sacrificed as much as I did.

"Let's not think of this day. You will always be my best friend. Even after…"

I meant to tell her how much I would still love her even after I died, but the words were stuck in my throat. It would make everything so much more real if I were to say it aloud. I couldn't bring myself to do it. She knew what I meant, however. I didn't need to say it.

Just having her in my arms was warming my heart. We broke the embrace and kept walking for a while in silence. We walked until we got to our favorite spot: the Sleeping Lake shores. Its waters were always calm and peaceful. The sun's rays reflected on the water, making it look like diamonds. We sat together in the grass, surrounded by trees, listening to the birds singing. A squirrel jumped joyfully on the grass nearby, searching for a nut or something to eat.

Kelly sighed as she stared at the water of the lake.

"You know… I've been thinking."

I turned to look at her, but she was still staring at the lake. She hesitated, then continued, "Since this is… well… Since you're turning twenty-six…."

She seemed to be searching for her words. It wasn't like her to hesitate, and I wondered what made her so reluctant. I grabbed her chin and gently turned her head my way.

"Say it. You know you can tell me anything."

Kelly's eyes sparkled, and she smiled.

"You know I can't resist your blue eyes when you look at me like that."

I chuckled. I knew the effect I had on her even though our affair was over. My lips curled up as I teased her, "Well then. Go ahead, speak."

She took a deep breath before speaking, staring into my eyes.

"I have been thinking that I would like to be your girl-friend. Even though it's only for a little while."

I stared at her in surprise. Kelly was gorgeous, and I appreciated her. But we both knew one day we'd meet our fated mates.

"You know it's not going to last long. My time is short."

She bit her lower lip.

"I know. That's why I want to make the most out of it."

"I would never want anything to ruin our friendship."

She nodded.

"I know. That's why we won't let it ruin our friendship. If anything happens, we'll go back to being best friends."

I weighed her words. It was only for a few months. I didn't want to lose what we had. Still, it would be nice to have a girlfriend again. It had been a while since I had one. Nights could get lonely. I would surely appreciate the warmth of a woman in my arms. The chances of me finding my fated mate were getting slimmer.

Before I could say anything, she added, "Of course, if you find your fated mate, we'll return to being best friends."

I snickered.

"At this point, I'm not sure it will happen before…."

She nodded.

"I know… But I know it's important to you."

My lips curved upwards. Kelly knew me so well. Finding my fated mate had been something important to me. As I was cursed to be sacrificed, I had hoped to be at least able to indulge in finding my fated mate. But as the years passed, I thought I might not have one. It would have been a cruel gift for my mate to be mated to someone destined to be killed at such a young age.

Kelly was still waiting for my answer, staring at me. I nodded to her.

"All right. If you think we can do this without screwing up our friendship, then let's do this."

She looked at me with the most beautiful smile ever, her eyes sparkling excitedly. "Are you sure?"

Instead of answering, I brought my lips to hers, sealing our deal with a kiss. Kelly put her hand behind my neck, holding me close to her. My tongue made its way through her parted lips. She tasted so good, and I couldn't help but grab her hips and bring her closer to me. She let out a small moan when we broke the kiss. I smirked as I replaced a fallen strand of hair behind her ear.

"This birthday is not that bad, after all."

We kissed for a while, then decided to return to the pack's house. I held her hand as we walked back. We didn't need to hide our relationship from anyone. I was happy I would spend this last year with Kelly. As we got close to the pack, I whispered in her ear.

"I was wondering if you'd like to come to my house tonight. We could shift and run together in the woods, then return to my room and enjoy the night."

Kelly had a devilish look on her face when she looked at me. Running together in our wolf form was one of the best ways to bond. Her wolf and mine would get to know each other, and even though we weren't fated mates, they would get closer. Things could get pretty intense, as our wolves tended to be wild and follow their instincts. After such a run, all our senses would be enhanced. This was promising to be an enjoyable night.

"Sure, I need to grab a few things at home."

Charles saluted us as we got back inside the wall. He stared at our locked hands but didn't say anything.

As we got close to the pack's house, Kelly got on her tiptoes and kissed me.

"I'll meet you back at your place later."

I let my lips linger on hers for a few seconds before whispering, "I'll be waiting for you."

I watched as she turned around and walked away. Her hips swayed from left to right, waking a hunger inside me.

As I was about to enter the pack's house, I saw Sherry walk to me, her auburn curly hair bouncing as she greeted me cheerfully. She was at least one head smaller than me.

"Matthew! I'm so glad to see you!"

Her hug was snuggling and motherly.

She looked up at me, exclaiming, "Happy birthday! Oh my gosh, I can't believe how fast you grew!"

I chuckled, "Thanks, Sherry. You know I stopped growing a while ago."

She smiled. "I know. But time passes too fast."

Then she raised a brow and added, "I saw you and Kelly. I didn't know you guys were dating?"

My lip curved upwards.

"Well, we only just started dating today."

"Didn't you guys used to date way back?"

I rubbed the back of my head.

"Yes, we used to, a few years ago. We've been only friends ever since. But it all changed this morning."

Sherry grinned widely. "Well, I'm happy for you both." Then she looked at her watch and added, "I need to go, the baby will wake up from his nap soon, and I'll need to feed him."

I chuckled, "Isn't your husband home?"

She nodded. "Yes, but the baby will only eat when I'm the one feeding him."

I smiled. "I guess he needs his mother's love."

Sherry smiled at my sentence. I added, "Thanks for coming and seeing me."

She waved. "You know I wouldn't have missed your birthday."

I watched her walk away, a warm feeling filling my heart. It was a nice motherly feeling.

I entered the pack's house feeling good. I heard voices arguing as I passed the strategic meeting room. I slowed and peeked inside to see my father fighting with Esme. They usually got along well. Curious, I stayed hidden and eavesdropped on their conversation.

"You're talking nonsense!" shouted Esme.

"Think about it! We could put an end to this!" answered my father.

"David, don't let your feelings get in the way of our pack's duties!"

"You know as well as me that everyone is tired of this!"

My father was walking furiously from one side of the room to another. Esme looked at the ceiling, shaking her head, letting out a breath of discouragement.

"Think of the consequences! The Moon Goddess would be furious with us!"

My dad swung his arm through the air.

"I'm tired of thinking of the consequences! I've seen two people get sacrificed already. Have you seen how they die? It needs to stop."

My heart skipped a beat. How did the people die when they got sacrificed? Ever since I was young, I knew I would be sacrificed one day. But no one ever told me how. Now thinking about it, it seemed weird that no one would mention it.

"I know damn well how they die. But you seem to forget that the Moon Goddess was the one to give us the task of guarding the demon's sepulcher. We're her wards, and we need to act accordingly!"

My dad stopped and stared at her threateningly.

"And *you* seem to forget that I'm the Alpha here."

Esme wasn't impressed by my father's display of authority. A spark flickered at the end of her fingers.

"Don't you forget that we don't abide by the Alpha rules here. We are a pack of werewolf-witches. I have a say in the pack's decisions as much as you do."

They stared into each other's eyes for a moment. I could feel the tension right up to where I was standing. I was holding my breath, not daring to move. I wasn't sure what was happening, but I knew it concerned me.

My dad finally stopped staring and let out a deep breath.

"I'm sorry, Esme. You're right. We are an amazing pack of werewolf-witches. For a moment, I forgot."

Esme's face softened, and the atmosphere lightened.

"Lucky I'm there to remind you."

My father looked disheartened. She gestured to him and hugged him.

"I understand your despair. Let's not make hasty decisions." She pondered for a moment, "Why don't we ask the pack? Let's vote on it. It's an important decision, and everyone should have their say in it."

My dad nodded to her before walking to stare outside the window.

"You're right. That's an excellent idea. Let's have an extraordinary meeting tomorrow."

He turned toward her. "Please, let everyone know they need to meet tomorrow night."

Esme nodded at him. She chanted a spell. Dozens of colorful fairies gathered before her, dust scattering on the ground as they flew around her. She gestured to them, and they all stopped, waiting for her to speak.

Only witches could talk to the fairies as it required them to imbue magic into their words for the fairies to understand. The same was true about understanding what the fairies said. I was always amazed to see witches talk to them.

"Go, gather everyone. Leave no one out. Tomorrow night, we have a meeting."

The fairies nodded, then flew away through the open window.

I waited a few seconds and walked past the room as casually as possible. I was eager for tomorrow's meeting. I wanted to know what this was all about. As I got to my room, I remembered that Kelly was coming. I decided not to think about the curse or the meeting today. I wanted to focus solely on her. Tonight was all about her and me.

I just got the time to clean my room before I heard her voice coming from the pack's hall.

"Hi David, hi Esme. I'm just going to see Matthew."

"Oh, I hadn't realized he was back!" Exclaimed Esme.

I smiled at that statement. Good, they were both lost in their thoughts and hadn't noticed me.

Kelly came into my room and dropped a small bag on the floor.

"Have you heard? Your father and Esme called an extraordinary meeting tomorrow night!"

I nodded to her and did as if I didn't know anything.

"Yes, I wonder what's it all about."

She had a disappointed look on her face.

"I hoped that you knew what it was about."

I chuckled as I wrapped my arms around her waist.

"Sorry to disappoint you."

She took a deep breath, her lips brushing against mine as she spoke.

"Hm… As long as you don't disappoint me tonight."

I couldn't help but smirk, a soft growl escaping my chest.

"You don't need to worry about that."

Serena's POV

The old house at the end of the pack's territory needed a lot of work. It was in shambles and threatened to crumble. The owner had called me at the right moment. Nothing could have been done to salvage the house if he had waited longer before contacting me.

I concentrated hard, casting all my energy on it. Slowly, I called forth the elements. The wood snapped back into place, the cracks disappearing as magic strengthened it, returning it to its former robustness. The fallen stones took back their place in the house structure. Plants grew and weaved themselves through the walls, strengthening the house further. Soon, you could have thought the home was new.

I panted from the effort, sweat beading on my forehead. A few people were clapping their hands.

"Wow!, Serena, you outdid yourself!"

Gregory was grinning, his blue eyes wide open, and his curly light brown hair fell slightly in his face. He was among the few in the pack to be born without a wolf or magic. He was also one of the most cheerful and friendly people I knew. I smiled at him.

"Thanks, Gregory!"

"It's not like *you* could have done that, Gregory!" shouted a teenager from behind. Gregory's face fell, and anger shot through me. I walked through the people in the crowd until I found two teenage boys laughing at their jokes.

"You think that's funny?" I asked, heat rising to my cheeks.

"Yeah!" laughed one of the boys.

"Didn't your parents teach you anything?"

"Like we'd listen!" huffed the second one.

"Members of the pack born without magic or wolves are as important as all the others," I gritted through my teeth.

They both laughed at what I said. Clearly, they needed to be taught some sense. I launched a tiny bolt of lightning at them, strong enough to sting a little but not to wound them. The first boy's wolf snarled at me.

"Hey!" they shouted. They weren't laughing anymore.

The first boy asked, "Are you looking for a fight?"

His wolf was growling at me. I smirked a flicker of lightning on the tip of my finger. "Think you can handle me?"

His face paled, and he took a step back. I added, "You two should get home and think about what I told you. Next time, I might even go talk to your parents myself."

The two of them stared at each other.

"You need to get some sense of humor," the first one said before leaving. The second one only stared at me briefly before following his friend.

I shook my head. I got back to Gregory, who stood there, not saying anything. I felt sad for him.

"Hey Gregory, sorry about that."

He rubbed the back of his neck, staring at the floor.

"That's okay. They're right."

I frowned. "No, they're not!"

His blue eyes stared into mine. They were shrouded by sadness, and I couldn't read the secrets they held.

"Well, I couldn't have repaired the house as you did."

It was true, but… "Still, it doesn't give them the right to mock you like they did."

Gregory hesitated for a moment, then said, "Thank you for defending me."

I smiled at him. "Of course! I had to!"

Mr. Gordon walked back slowly, staring at his house.

"You're really the best spell caster!" he exclaimed in awe. I grinned at him. I took a deep breath as I stared at the house. I had to admit it looked nice. Warmth spread to my cheeks as I admired my work proudly.

"Don't wait that long the next time you need repairs. I couldn't have repaired it if it had collapsed."

Mr. Gordon replaced the glasses on his nose.

"I had barely noticed. My neighbor was the one to tell me to call you."

I refrained from laughing at the fact that maybe Mr. Gordon needed new glasses.

"You should thank your neighbor, then."

The old man nodded to me and turned to admire his house once again. Just then, a group of fairies flew around us. They were talking to us. Werewolves couldn't communicate with them, but all the witches could. I gasped when they told us an extraordinary pack meeting would be held tomorrow. Something significant must be happening for our grand witch and the Alpha to summon everyone. A knot formed in my stomach as I related the news to the werewolves around me. I hoped it was nothing terrible.

Gregory had the same look as me on his face.

"It must be something important."

I nodded. "Let's hope it's good news."

He nodded, but I couldn't help but think he was still shaken by what had happened earlier.

"Are you going back home?" I asked him. He lived a few houses further than mine, so we could walk back together.

Gregory stared absently at the void in front of him. His lips were moving, but he wasn't saying anything. Finally, he snapped out of it, mumbling, "Huh, no. I'll go… I'll take a walk… I think."

I felt tired after all that house renovations and decided to get home. I watched Gregory wander in the forest. I wondered if I should go after him for a moment, but then I decided maybe he needed to be alone.

It was already late afternoon when I got out of the shower. Knowing we had a pack meeting tomorrow night was making me nervous. But I knew the perfect way not to think about it. I got my hair into a bun and made a hot cup of coffee before sinking into my favorite chair with a blanket. It might be summer, but evenings could get chilly. These were the perfect evenings: my favorite book, a blanket, and a coffee.

Chapter 2 (DeMörder)

Missing

The soft veil of darkness surrounded me. I panted as I shoved the knife into the man's chest once more. Blood splattered on my face. I loved the foul metallic smell of it. He had fought well and ruined one of my favorite shirts in the process. It was torn and stained with blood. It's only fair that I prevailed. At least my favorite shirt wouldn't be ruined for nothing. I dug my fingers into the still-warm flesh, feeling his organs around. It had a distinctive, somewhat satisfying feel. It was my first time killing someone, and I must admit that I enjoyed it.

But first things first. I needed to see if he had told me the truth. I wiped my knife's blade on the man's clothes, put it back into its sheath, and stood. I concentrated on the corpse. At first, nothing happened, and I wondered if I had been lied to again. But as I continued, a dark force ran through my body, draining my energy. I panted from the effort and leaned on a tree to keep from falling. I would need to think of a way to replenish my life force if I was to survive.

I kept pushing, feeling my life force and what made me a human being drain as I did. Suddenly, the arms and legs of the corpse started moving. He slowly rose from the dead, blood pooling from his open wound as he did. I watched in awe as the man I had just killed was now standing in front of me. It was a beauty, like a second coming to life.

His brown hair was damp with blood sticking to his skin. His brown eyes were staring at the void before him, but I felt he was staring at me, nonetheless, waiting for an order. Questions filled my mind. Did he remember his past life? Was he the same person? Was there a soul in his body? I wish I had been given more details when I received this power.

"Can you talk?" I asked.

The dead man only grunted. I guess he couldn't. I wondered how strong he was. Was he able to follow simple orders?

I pointed to a medium-sized rock. Something a human was able to lift.

"Grab that rock over there."

The man slowly turned toward the rock. He walked to it, limping on his limbs as he did. He crouched to the ground and quickly picked it up.

"Good." I rubbed my hands together. "Go grab this one, now," I ordered, pointing to a bigger rock I couldn't lift. The dead man threw the first rock to the floor. I was amazed to see him effortlessly lift the second rock. With that much power, anything was possible. So… the demon had told the truth. All that was left now…

"Go! Find me some men and women to strengthen our forces! Bring them to me."

The man grunted and started walking in the direction of the nearest town. This was perfect! He would be pleased with my progress, and I would get what I wanted. Finally! After all these years…

Matthew's POV

The night felt warm as we stood outside, near the house. Surrounded by thick bushes and cedars, we were hidden away from prying eyes. It was my favorite spot to change into my wolf. Not that there were a lot of people watching, anyway. I turned to Kelly. Her eyes flickered, watching me. I knew it was her wolf; she wanted out. My wolf growled softly in response, making Kelly smile.

I removed Kelly's shirt, brushing my fingers on her soft skin. She looked deliciously tempting, but I would be patient. She helped me get naked as I helped remove her clothes too. Her nails brushed on my skin, making goosebumps appear as they roamed my chest. I was already hard in anticipation, but my wolf was screaming to get out. I had to get him free first. I grabbed her hand, kissing each of her knuckles, and whispered, "You little minx, wait till I take care of you."

The devilish smile on her face told me she knew exactly what she was doing. I kissed Kelly's soft lips, grabbing the back of her head and bringing her close to me. Her scent of peaches was intoxicating. She moaned into the kiss, her nipples brushing on my chest.

I stared into her eyes. "Ready?"

She grinned. "You know I am."

I smirked. I could smell the scent of her arousal. Without further words, I let this marvelous feeling take hold of me, giving control to my wolf. I felt my senses heighten as the shift was completed.

Kelly's small gray wolf was looking at me passionately. My wolf swelled with pride as she rubbed her muzzle on mine, mixing our scents. Every wolf would be able to smell my scent on her as well. As the Alpha's son, no one would dare to take what's mine.

I gestured toward the woods. She nodded at me, then started running into the forest. My wolf let out a slight growl and took off after her. Her scent was easy to follow, mingling with the wind as I ran through the dew-dampened grass. Adrenaline pumped through my veins, making the game much more fun. I quickly caught up to her. I was of Alpha blood; my wolf was bigger and faster than hers. My wolf howled when I got to Kelly, and her wolf howled in answer. Soon, I was pinning her to the ground, displaying my strength to her. Her wolf only stared back at mine in the most enticing way. We played in the grass for a while, a display of force and affection that felt exhilarating.

I could feel my wolf growing restless from the closeness of Kelly's wolf. Desire rose within me, heightened by my wolf's senses. It was becoming overwhelming. I knew what my wolf wanted, and I wanted it too, but not in my wolf's form.

I gestured toward the house. Kelly's wolf's eyes were heavy with desire as well. We eagerly ran back home to where we had left our clothes.

The shift back to my human form came fast. My wolf and I were both eager for what came next. As I stared back at Kelly's naked body, I knew I wouldn't make it back to my bed. She moaned when my lips met hers. Breathless, heavy with desire, hidden from prying eyes, I laid her gently on the ground under the starry night.

Serena's POV

It was early morning. The birds chirped happily in the trees, and the sun was already warm. However hard I tried, I couldn't stop thinking about tonight's meeting. I was curious to know what it was about, but I couldn't shake this bad feeling creeping on me. Something terrible was bound to happen. I didn't know if it was because of tonight's meeting or something else, but I was sure of it.

When I was a kid, I used to have premonitory dreams. My mother kept telling me they were only dreams. No witch ever had the power to predict the future. Only the oracle could, but there hadn't been an oracle in centuries. This power was thought to be lost forever. But I knew what I saw in my dreams. Everything was so clear and well-defined! Sure enough, it would occur precisely how I had seen it a few days later. Now that I was an adult, the dreams had faded and didn't occur as often, but they still occasionally happened. Nonetheless, this bad feeling wasn't just an impression.

I finally decided to see if I could help people in the pack while waiting for the extraordinary session to start. Charles waved at me as I exited my house. I watched him go to the training grounds with the other pack's guards. Just as I got to my neighbor's house, a woman ran into the streets. Her long red hair swung as she screamed around, "Please! Has anyone seen my husband?"

She wasn't a member of our pack. She looked tired and distressed, and I couldn't sense any magic in her. If I had to guess, she was a human from the town to the north. People gathered around her. I grabbed her hands.

"Calm down. Who's your husband? What does he look like?"

Her green eyes stared into mine as she took a moment to catch her breath.

"His name is Gerald. He has brown hair and brown eyes."

Some people whispered to one another. This could be about anyone, and I knew no one named Gerald.

"What makes you think he's here?"

"He loves to hunt. He told me about this place. Said people with magic lived here. He has a friend living here, so I thought maybe he was with you."

I had no idea whom she was talking about. I knew that a few humans were aware of us. Although we preferred to remain hidden, we sometimes befriended humans.

A man at the back said, "I think I know who she's talking about. A good fellow. He hunts with Tarriel sometimes. I haven't seen him lately, though."

The woman stared back at me, her eyes pleading. "Please, you have to help me!"

I couldn't leave her like that. I loved helping people as much as I could. I loved to think that I could make a difference in someone's life.

"Let's see if we can find him. When was the last time you saw him?"

She put a hand on her belly, thinking. "He went hunting last night. He's been hunting a lot lately, trying to make some money for when our baby comes. He hasn't come back. That's not like him to disappear without saying anything."

My heart sank when I realized she was pregnant and the father, her partner, was missing. Growing up, I was so close to my dad that I couldn't imagine this child growing up without one.

"What's your name?"

"Odilia."

"Come with me, Odilia. Let's see if we can find your husband."

She nodded, and her face showed the hint of a smile. I didn't know if I could help her find her husband, but I knew Esme would surely be able to do it. Her wisdom was great, and her knowledge was vast.

As we walked toward Esme's house, Odilia looked everywhere with great interest.

"Is it true you people have magic? You don't look any different than me."

I nodded. "Yes, it is. Some of us have great powers, but some don't."

She frowned. "That's sad. I guess they must feel pretty left out."

I shook my head. "Everyone in the pack plays an important role. Even those without magic."

"What do you mean by 'pack'?"

I smirked. "I guess you don't know. Some of us are born with a wolf inside."

She stopped walking for a moment, her mouth agape.

"A wolf? For real? Are you guys werewolves? Does it have a life of its own? How does that even work?"

I giggled. I loved how curious Odilia was about us. We talked as we walked, and I explained to her as much as possible. I tried to keep it simple, as it was a lot for her to take in. The fact she was open-minded made it easier for her to accept what I was telling her.

Esme was outside her house when we arrived, tending to her garden. Her long white hair was braided and fell over her left shoulder, down to her hips. She wore her usual light gray dress and a belt of fresh woven plants. Bent over her flowers and vegetable garden, she was imbuing magic into the plants, the air glowing green around them. She was giving them energy, making them grow tall and strong. It was one of Esme's talents. She was one of the best gardeners of the pack.

Odilia gasped when she saw her.

"What is she doing?"

I smirked. "She's helping the plants grow."

Her eyes widened. "Is she making them grow faster? Can she turn a seed into a tree in a matter of minutes?"

I giggled and shook my head. "Not exactly. She's providing them with everything they need to grow strong. Think of it like a magical fertilizer."

She gasped in awe. Just then, Esme turned and smiled when she saw us. She stopped casting her spell, the air returning to normal as she came to meet us.

"Hi there, my sweet Serena. To what pleasure do I owe your visit? Who is your friend here?"

"This is Odilia. She's a human from the town to the north. She's searching for her husband."

Esme frowned at my words and asked Odilia, "I'm sorry. When was the last time you saw him?"

"He left last night to hunt. I figured he might be here."

Esme didn't understand, so I added, "Someone said that he sometimes hunts with Tarriel."

Odilia nodded. "He spoke to me before about this town. I mean, this pack. But it's the first time I've come here."

Esme grabbed Odilia's hands in hers and squeezed them.

"Come, let's see if we can find where your husband is."

We followed Esme inside her house to a room filled with potions, reagents, and animal bones. Fresh plants and flowers hung from the ceiling, left to dry. The scent of spices and the odor of various plants and flowers gave a pleasant smell to the room. Multiple windows let the sun's light illuminate the room. A beautiful rainbow pattern caught my eye, painted by the sun rays passing through a quartz gem in front of one of the windows.

Esme probably had been collecting herbs all her life. I had never seen such an extensive collection anywhere in the pack. Being a witch myself, I could only watch in awe. I couldn't even name all of them, but I hoped to have my collection of rare, powerful components one day. Although, potion making wasn't my strongest point. I was born a very gifted spell caster. I still enjoyed brewing potions once in a while.

Esme grabbed a small black cauldron and summoned a flame underneath it. She stared around the room, grabbed a few leaves here and there, and threw them into the pot. I was amazed to see the cauldron's surface glowing as the solution heated up. A scent of cinnamon and nutmeg floated from the cauldron, reminding me of the smell of apple pies.

Soon, I could watch my reflection on the liquid's surface. As Esme concentrated and recited a spell, the surface blurred and became a mixture of diffused colors. A frown formed on Esme's face. She tried her spell a few times and waited a few minutes, but nothing happened.

She spoke with a hint of surprise, "That's strange. I can't pinpoint the location of your husband."

Odilia covered her mouth with her hand. Her voice was shaky as she asked, "Does it mean he's…?"

She didn't finish her sentence, but her watery eyes made it clear what she was thinking.

I knew it wasn't good that Esme couldn't find Odilia's husband. Judging by Esme's reaction, I'd say I was probably right, but she tried to reassure Odilia.

"It's possible a spell shrouds his location."

Odilia relaxed at those words, but I didn't. I still understood what was left unsaid by Esme. A spell shrouding his location was only one of the possible reasons she couldn't find him. The other reasons were grimmer, and I tried not to consider them.

"Do you know how we could get past this spell?" asked Odilia, clinging to what little hope she had left.

Esme shook her head. "I'm afraid the only thing we can do is wait and see if the spell fades."

Odilia frowned. "I hope it won't be too long. I need him with me."

"We could also send someone to look for him," I suggested.

"But no one knows what he looks like," answered Esme.

"People said Tarriel knows him," I reminded her.

Odilia suddenly lost balance and fell to the floor. Luckily, I could cast a wind spell underneath her just before she hit the floor, cushioning her fall with air. I quickly grabbed her in my arms, seeing she was unconscious. Esme grabbed a cloth and summoned a rain cloud to get it wet. Gently, she wiped Odilia's forehead.

My thoughts raced as Odilia still didn't wake up. I frantically searched for a spell I could cast to make her feel better.

"Should I cast a healing spell? What's happening to her?"

Esme remained calm; years of experience had taught her how to react in such a situation. She examined Odilia, taking in her vital signs.

"She had a pressure drop, nothing serious. She doesn't need a healing spell."

Just as she spoke those words, Odilia started returning to her senses. She blinked her eyes slowly. Her voice was weak.

"What… What happened?"

Esme answered, "Your pressure dropped, and you fainted."

Odilia winced. "This has been happening more and more since I got pregnant."

I slowly sat her on the ground. She put her hands on the floor as if to stabilize herself.

"My head is still spinning a little."

Esme had a pensive look on her face, staring at the air.

"You say it started when you got pregnant?"

Odilia nodded.

Esme asked carefully, hesitating, "Is Gerald… Is Gerald a human?"

I was shocked at what Esme's question implied. Could it be that Gerald was a werewolf? Or a witch, maybe? Or maybe something else… There'd been reports of demons and other creatures hiding as humans. Some simply wanted to live a simple life, blending with humans harmoniously. Others were living a murderous life at night.

Odilia's eyes widened. "Of course he is!"

Esme had a doubtful look on her face. I trusted her wisdom more than anything. She plastered a fake smile and answered, "Of course! What was I thinking?"

Then she turned to me. "Serena, prepare the bed in my guest room. Odilia can stay there for a while."

I had known Esme for years. I knew she was hiding something, but I couldn't ask.

"What?" Odilia asked, surprised.

Esme answered in a maternal tone, "You are too weak to go back alone."

Reluctantly, Odilia nodded.

Esme added, "You must stay here until you are better or until we find your husband."

Odilia seemed lost in her thoughts for a moment before seemingly accepting Esme's offer, not that she had a choice. She wasn't even up and about again, much less able to return to the human town.

"Thank you for your hospitality."

I left the room while Esme and Odilia were talking to-gether. The guest room was at the back of the house. The room was empty most of the time. A weathering spell had been cast on the furniture, keeping it at the size of a bullet so the space could be used for something else.

Rows of shelves packed with books filled the room. Esme had all the best spellbooks! Some were very ancient, and the pleasant smell of old paper filled the air. I smiled as I summoned a magical chest. In one simple spell, all the books flew into the trunk. Although there were dozens of books, the chest's interior would stretch to accommodate everything you put inside while keeping its original size outside. I then shrunk the shelves and stuffed them into the trunk as well. All that was left now was to return the room's furniture to its original size.

"Reverti, regressus, reversio."

In the blink of an eye, a nice bed filled the room, perfectly made. To the side was a dresser filled with clothes and personal items for the guest.

When I returned to see Esme, Odilia was standing, holding Esme's hand for balance.

"Serena, perfect timing! Come, help me get Odilia to her room."

I grabbed Odilia's other hand and slowly walked toward the guest room. She seemed more stable than earlier, and her face was less pale, but I could see she was still fragile. She smiled when we sat her on the bed, looking around everywhere, taking in the room where she would stay.

Esme smiled. "Take it easy. You can use whatever you want in this room."

"Really?" asked Odilia, surprised.

"Yes. The bathroom is just across the hall. You will find everything you need to take a bath."

Odilia smiled at those words.

"Oh, a relaxing bath sounds delightful!"

"Good. I need to prepare for the pack's meeting."

I jumped at these words. Was it time already? I had almost forgotten about it!

"Can I come?" asked Odilia.

Esme shook her head.

"You're still too weak, my dear. But rest assured, we will only discuss pack matters and nothing that should worry you."

Odilia nodded. Esme added, "I have already sent a fairy to find Tarriel. I have also sent another to get a warm meal for you. I will be back late tonight."

Odilia nodded again. "Thank you again for everything. I don't know how to repay your kindness."

"There's nothing to repay, my child. Now, rest."

That being said, we exited the room. Tarriel arrived just as we got back to the front of the house. He was among the few to be born with a wolf and magic. He was one of the best hunters of the pack. I loved how he kept his long red hair braided and the piney smell from his thick beard.

"You wanted to see me, Esme?" he asked humbly.

"Yes, do you know of a man named Gerald?"

Tarriel thought for a second.

"Oh yes! Gerald. A nice man and a very talented hunter! More than most men I know."

"He's been missing."

Tarriel clenched his jaw. "That can't be good."

"His wife is here, searching for him," Esme added.

"He has a wife? I didn't know. Well, not that it matters…," he muttered.

"Could you look for him?"

"Sure, I know all his favorite hunting spots."

"Thank you!" Esme answered.

Tarriel nodded and left, eager to find Gerald.

I was relieved that he had agreed to look for him. Being one of the pack's best hunters, I couldn't imagine a better person to look for the man.

I turned to Esme. Now that we were alone, I asked, "Do you really believe Gerald isn't human?"

Esme nodded.

"There's a good chance. There have been records of humans struggling to adapt to the fast-growing rhythm of werewolf babies. Especially if the mating bond has not been established."

I thought for a moment. The mate bond was when the male bit the female in the neck. At this moment, the werewolf's genes would partly transfer to the female, making her compatible with him so they could reproduce. It was common knowledge among packs. Preferably, we would wait to find our fated mates. But when werewolves decided to form a couple, they would bond together, sealing their destiny. A bond would form, even if they weren't fated mates. Although nothing was stronger than the fated mate's bond. The breaking of the mate bond could be very painful. Fated mates usually stayed together for life as they could never recover entirely from breaking the bond. Not that they wanted to separate; fated mates were drawn to one another like magnets. But sometimes, one member of the couple would die too soon, leaving the other with an eternal life of grief and suffering. Witches worked the same way since we were a hybrid pack.

Esme continued, "The fact she said he was human means he never bit her. So either he is a werewolf and never told her the truth, or he is human, and she's simply sick. But my gut tells me it's the former."

I gasped at this possibility.

"But I thought werewolves and humans couldn't reproduce without the bond!"

Esme nodded. "This is true, though I will search my books to see if I can find a case like hers. For now, only time will tell if we can discover the truth."

I nodded, my mind full of questions about the implications of a werewolf and a human creating a pup without being bonded.

Esme showed me the door.

"Please go; I must get to the pack's hall to prepare for the meeting."

I snapped back to reality at those words. The meeting! I was eager to know what this was all about. I needed to prepare too. I nodded to Esme and left her house.

Chapter 3 (Matthew)

Harvester of death

I had spent the day with Kelly. Although our relationship was new, it felt natural since I had known her for so many years. We were only kids when she joined our pack with her mom. I still remember how her mother used to braid her hair in two braids falling on either side of her face. Her mother was Jack's fated mate. She had left Kelly's father and moved into our pack. I instantly became friends with Kelly. Growing up, there was always a clear attraction between us. When I turned eighteen, we were both disappointed to realize we weren't fated mates. That's the main reason we ended our affair.

She turned to me, smiling from the excitement.

"It's almost time for the meeting! Aren't you excited to know what it's all about?"

Excited wasn't the right word. The meeting couldn't start soon enough. I was dying to know what my father wanted to say. I knew it concerned me. I wrapped my arms around Kelly, the peachy scent of her skin filling my nose. I took a deep breath, letting the hot air roll on her neck as I exhaled, making goosebumps appear. She rested her head on my chest. The heat from her body felt good against mine. It reminded me of last night and how good it felt to have a woman in my arms when I woke up this morning. I kissed the top of her head.

"Yes. I can't wait to see what this meeting will be about."

"Do you think we should go now?"

I checked the clock. It was almost time.

"Sure, let's see if my father needs help to set up the room."

I squeezed her in my arms, leaving a trail of kisses on her neck before we exited my room.

Rows of chairs had been set in the meeting room. The big wooden desk had been pushed to the back to make more space. The chandeliers that hung from the wooden beams in the ceiling had been lit. A few magical light spheres were also lit to make the room brighter. Mr. Gordon was already there, leaning on his cane.

"This better be good. I had to cancel my bingo to be here," he grumbled to Esme while replacing his glasses.

She shook her head, looking at the old man. Although Esme was the oldest of the pack, she was still the one that taught magic classes to the young ones. She was respected by all, one of the most powerful witches, and took part in the decision-making of the pack with my father.

"Please, Mr. Gordon. I know it's a last-minute meeting, but this is an extraordinary session."

The old man slowly walked away, mumbling. Kelly shook her head, laughing, "Oh, Mr. Gordon will never change! I'll go cheer him up."

She squeezed my hand, then ran up to Mr. Gordon. I watched the old man's mood lighten as he talked with Kelly. A strong hand fell on my shoulder.

"You have a wonderful girlfriend, Son."

I turned to see my father smiling. My lips curved up.

"Thanks, dad."

"Is she your mate?"

I shook my head.

"No, she isn't. I would have liked it, but the Moon Goddess decided otherwise."

He nodded. "Either way, it's nice to have her around."

I grinned. My father was right; Kelly had a way of lighting up a room just by being there.

"Do you need help with anything?"

My father shook his head.

"No, thanks. I have everything I need. We just need to wait for everyone to arrive."

I nodded to him. A knot formed in my stomach, and I almost asked him if I could know what the meeting was about. Then I remembered I wasn't supposed to have heard anything about it, so I shouldn't be so anxious. My father was still staring at me. His stare was filled with hidden words. For a moment, I felt he wanted to tell me something. He let out a long breath and put both hands on my shoulders.

"Whatever happens tonight, know I love you dearly, my son."

His words were heavy with meaning. I wanted to ask what he meant, but he was gone before I could ask. People started to fill the room, and as the pack's Alpha, my father had to greet them. I was left alone to wonder what he meant, but I figured I would know soon enough.

The room quickly filled with every wolf, witch, and human from the pack. Everyone was talking, eager to know what the meeting was about. The air felt too hot, with everyone pressed against each other. I was startled when two hands grabbed my hips. A sense of relief brushed over me when I turned around and realized it was Kelly, her crystal laughter resonating through the chaos and noise that filled the room.

"Did I scare you?"

My wolf growled a little. He didn't want to look weak in front of her.

"You only surprised me," I retorted.

Kelly's eyes flickered. I could feel her wolf enjoying the scare that she had given me. But Kelly's smile showed her true thoughts.

"I'm only teasing you."

Kelly cuddled into my arms, her body's warmth radiating through mine as she did. She was my beacon in this sea of chaos. A soft purr resonated from her wolf, and a teasing smile appeared. My wolf purred back at hers in contentment.

"It's starting. I wanted to make sure to be with you."

I wrapped my arms around her and squeezed her affectionately. Kissing her neck, I whispered in her ear, "Thanks."

My father stepped on a wooden bench to get everyone's attention. Beside him was Esme, standing solemnly. Usually, no one talks at the same time as the Alpha, but today's meeting was so unusual that people didn't even pay attention to my father. He cleared his throat. People up front stopped talking, but people in the back didn't hear him.

He spoke loudly with a strong voice, "Everyone! Listen up!"

People finally heard him and stopped talking, and I was glad my father didn't resort to using his Alpha's authority on the pack. I was proud to say my dad was an incredible Alpha, loved by his pack. I knew he had the strength to assert his will if needed, but he only used it in extreme cases.

The room was silent, everyone staring at my father, waiting expectantly.

"Thank you for gathering on such short notice," he started. "We have an urgent matter to discuss."

He took a slight pause, scanning the room with his eyes.

"As you all know, my son, Matthew, has turned twenty-six years old. As the chosen one, he is bound to be sacrificed the day Eurynomos's seal weakens."

I felt the weight of everyone's stare on me. I didn't need a reminder of my upcoming death and wondered why my father was bringing this up. My heartbeat increased, and I could crumble with embarrassment as I was the center of everyone's attention. Kelly squeezed my hands, making me relax a little.

He continued, "The weight of this curse has hung over our pack for generations, each time harder to bear than the last."

One of the old pack members shouted, "I still remember when my sweet Jessica left us! It was cruel and devastating!"

My father glanced at me for a moment before looking back at everyone. I swallowed hard. Jessica was the last member of the pack to be born on a blessed night. I wasn't born when it happened, but I had heard stories of her. Although none of the stories ever told how the chosen one died. The fact he had just said her death was cruel and devastating made me churn. Was he referring to the way she died? Or to the fact that he lost his daughter?

My father continued, "Exactly! And so, after talking with Esme, we have come to you with a proposal. As a pack, we will leave this place, give up our job as the Moon Goddess's wards, and become a rogue pack."

My heart skipped a beat at those words. What he was proposing was outrageous. Yet, this meant I wouldn't need to die this year. It opened a lot of possibilities for me. My wolf was wagging his tail at these thoughts. The whispers coming from everyone quickly brought me back to reality. What my father was implying was also heavy with consequences.

"What about the Moon Goddess? Wouldn't she be mad?" shouted one man.

"What will happen to the demon?" asked another.

"You're blinded because of your son!" shouted a woman.

Questions and accusations came from everywhere. Some were happy with the idea, but a lot were wary. I couldn't blame them. I felt terrible and didn't dare say anything. It wasn't my call, and I was afraid to receive threats if I were to say anything.

The silence came back when Esme stepped forward.

"We don't have the answers to all your questions. We don't know what will happen to the demon or if the Goddess will be furious at us. We know this is a big decision, so we decided the whole pack should vote together on this."

Whispers filled the room again.

The man that had spoken earlier shouted, "Well, if it does anything to prevent what happened to my sweet Jessica from happening to anyone else, then I'm in."

Some cheered him, but others shouted, "We can't betray the Goddess!"

The man added, "What if your unborn child is the next sacrifice? What if it's your grandchild? How would you like that?"

Some people looked at the floor when they heard him. He was really good at selling the idea!

He added, "Even if it's not your child, are you okay, knowing one of our members needs to be sacrificed? Someone who might not have found love yet. Someone who could have done so much more with his life. Do you even know the painful way the chosen one dies?"

The room went silent, and once again, I froze. The more I heard about it, the more I wondered why no one had ever said anything to me about it.

My father spoke, "They don't know. Only the Alpha, the grand witch, and the parents, if they wish, can watch when the chosen one is sacrificed."

The words got out before I could contain them, "Why hasn't anyone spoken to me about this before? I feel like I should have the right to know the way I'm going to be sacrificed."

My father had a guilty look on his face. He didn't speak, and the air felt heavy. Esme put her hand on his arm, speaking softly, "We don't say it to the chosen one, not to scare him. The ritual is kept secret. The fewer people know about it, the better."

"But it won't matter anymore!" said the old man. "After tonight, there won't be any sacrifices anymore! It will have ended with my sweet Jessica."

More people cheered him, and fewer objected. My father looked at me as if to say something, then quickly got back to everyone.

"Let's take a vote. All in favor of stopping this curse and becoming a rogue pack; raise your hand."

I watched nervously as some hands started to rise in the air. Kelly raised her hand, motioning for me to do the same. Some people looked around, unsure. Now that more than half the people had their hands in the air, they decided to get theirs too. As people looked around, the few who still hadn't raised their hands finally decided to give in to the popular pressure.

My father was smiling at me, his hand in the air, a single tear rolling down his cheek.

He asked, "Anyone against?"

All the hands went down. Everyone looked at each other, silently waiting to see if someone would vote against the motion. I waited nervously, wondering if someone would dare to raise his hand. After a few minutes, when it was clear no one would oppose, my father whispered, "Thank you, everyone."

Kelly hugged me while my brain failed to process what had happened. I knew I was supposed to be happy, but I was shocked. I had accepted my death from the moment I was old enough to comprehend the Goddess's curse. Never had I thought it would be lifted. I returned Kelly's hug. This meant I would get to spend more time with her, and I couldn't be happier. My heart beat fast. I now had years ahead of me to appreciate my life.

Esme took the lead, as my father couldn't contain his emotions.

"We will need a few days to prepare everything. We welcome everyone's help. We have a lot to do."

A man stepped forward. "I'll help!"

It was Gregory. His curly brown hair was strewn with dirt, and his clothes were torn and dirty. He looked like a mess, frankly.

A few teenagers giggled, and one shouted, "You can't even do anything in the pack! You're just useless."

Another girl added, "Yeah! Good-for-nothing! Born without a wolf and without magic. You're so pathetic!"

They started chanting, "Hopeless Gregory smells like pee!"

Gregory only stood there, not answering anything. His blue eyes were filled with sadness, staring at the void before him. All around him, people watched but didn't say anything. Anger rose in me. Just as I felt I could burst if I stayed there any longer, not saying anything, my father sent a wave of his Alpha's powers to the group of teenagers. They immediately stopped and fell to the floor.

He growled, "I don't want to hear anyone say to humans they are useless!"

People trembled with fear from the anger carried by his words.

"Every member of the pack is important. Even if they're born without a wolf or magic. Am I making myself clear?" The teenagers nodded. Gregory was smiling.

My father released his Alpha's power, letting the teenagers move again. None of them dared to look at him directly.

"Thank you for your help, Gregory. I will find something you can help with."

A feeling of relief washed over me. I still couldn't believe I wouldn't need to die this year. This was amazing, and I would need some time to really comprehend what it meant to me. I also wanted to know more about the sacrifice ritual, even though I wouldn't need to go through it. But none of that mattered now that Kelly was squeezing my hand, her peachy scent intoxicating me as she lovingly whispered, "Come on, let's go home."

I followed her, eager to sprinkle kisses on her body and love her in all the ways she loved.

DeMörder's POV

*** A few days later ***

How long had it been since my first kill? Two weeks? Maybe more? Time was slipping away more and more as I felt my sanity leave my grasp. I had frequent blackouts and couldn't remember where I had been yesterday. Every now and then, I would watch myself from afar. The line between reality and dream was getting thinner. I often found myself waking up in strange places I didn't remember going to. Still, this dark bond was a gift, and I wouldn't let go of it. But it was draining me, pulling me toward Death's cold hands. As I bent the rules of the living and the dead, toying with the Gods' powers, I feared my own death only more. I knew my soul wouldn't find rest in the afterlife, not after the deal I had made with the demon. I had no intention of dying anytime soon. Not before I asserted my vengeance, anyway. I still needed to fill my end of the bargain with the demon: kill as many people as possible and revive them to join my army. It should be easy enough.

Luckily, I had found a useful way to regenerate myself when I inadvertently used my powers on a living human. Concentrating on this woman who was spitting insults at me after abducting her, I was able to drain her life force, replenishing mine. The scream that filled the air as I sucked the life out of her was shrilling. It served her right for being so insolent with me. I can still remember the look of incomprehension on her face as she was slowly dying. Filled with this newfound ability, I could now use my powers without fear of dying. I felt like a God, giving people what they deserved for their sins. I was the judge and the executioner.

My army of zombies was growing. They couldn't talk; they mindlessly executed any tasks I asked of them and were re-animated from the dead, so I figured it was an appropriate name. That's how I decided to call my reanimated corpses anyway. There were so many of them that I had to find a hideout. We couldn't stay in the open fields anymore. I walked to the southwest and finally stumbled on a crescent moon-shaped cliff. Its walls rose feet up in the sky, and the point of its walls almost touched, making for a very narrow entrance to the rocky area. At the base of the cliff was a dark coniferous forest. It wasn't completely closed like a cavern, but I liked the open sky, allowing me to see the moonlight glowing. The night was a constant reminder of my task since the ones bringing the night were the ones I had bonded with. Overall, it made the area an excellent place to make my hideout.

I have noticed that the forest has been slowly dying since I stayed here with my zombies. The coniferous trees turned black, and deciduous trees have lost their leaves. The bark has died and turned black. Only the roots of the trees and the dirt remain on the ground. The dark energy used to raise the dead leeched the life from the forest. Not that I really care about the forest anyway, but it's the best explanation I could come up with. As nature died slowly, I felt my domain was expanding, giving me control over life.

"Harvester of death."

My eyes fell on the man kneeling in front of me. He was one of the few I hadn't killed. Their number was growing. By choosing servitude and worship, they were allowed to stay alive. The only difference between them and my zombies was that I could converse with them. They consciously chose to worship me instead of being mindless slaves controlled by my powers. Still, I couldn't deny that I liked having worshippers. They were handy and worked restlessly at finding recruits for our group. Fear and the promise of power kept them loyal. Together, we would right what is wrong in this world. When it would be done, and my vengeance is asserted, I will see what to do with them. Who knows, I might even find a use for them. If not, I'll dispose of them.

I replaced the crown on my head. It was nothing fancy, but my worshippers had built it from animal horns and metal. It was only fitting that their master had a crown. I thanked them and imbued it with dark magic, giving it a dim blueish glow.

"What is it?"

The man raised his eyes from the ground but didn't dare to make eye contact with me. His frail body shook from fear and respect.

"The recruits have arrived."

I smirked. "You did well, Marcus."

The man slightly bowed his head, then walked to the side. I walked from my chamber to the throne room. It was a vast rocky plateau. A part of it was elevated. That's where I had created my rocky throne, carved into a massive boulder with my dark powers. It had been burdensome, and I had to suck the life force of two grown men to recharge myself, but what were two lives? No God would live without a throne, and so I had to have one. These two men should be proud to have served such a holy purpose.

The floor stayed elevated for a few feet past my throne, separating my worshippers and me. Then it dropped in a stair-like manner.

Down on the floor below were two women and one man. Their hands were tied, and my worshippers held down their faces.

"Bow to the Harvester of death!" one of my followers shouted.

"Let go of me, you freak!" screamed one of the women.

Her blonde hair was dirty and tangled. Blood was dripping down on the floor beneath her face, and I could smell the distinctive stench of resilience. She wouldn't accept defeat, and I hated people with the guts to defy me. She was struggling to get up, trying to get her hands free. I watched as my follower, Judah, fought to keep her down. Just then, the woman gave a headbutt to Judah, pushing through with all her force and getting to her feet. The other tied man and woman looked up in surprise. A few other followers and zombies moved to catch the woman.

Surrounded, it didn't take much time for them to catch her. Judah walked furiously toward her, wiping blood on his chin just as they caught her. He grabbed the woman's hair as he reached her and slapped her face hard, the woman's groan filling the air as he did. He then proceeded to beat her again and again, never having enough. Pleasure filled me with each of her screams, and the sight of her blood excited me. Judah was one of my favorite worshippers and one of my most loyal. He had lived a life of hardships and would be greatly rewarded when I ruled. But I didn't want him to kill her before I had decided what to do with her.

"Enough!" I shouted sternly.

Everyone froze, staring at me in silence. Although I wanted to rip the woman's eyes out from the insolence she had shown, I figured she might be useful. A high-spirit follower could kill enthusiastically or move mountains if she decided to follow. I walked up to her, my footsteps echoing on the walls as people stared at me silently.

I asked her, "You! What's your name?"

She spat in defiance, blood mixed with her spit. Her dirty hair partially hid her green eyes, but I could still read their fury. In the flash of a second, a vision flooded my brain; the image of digging my fingers into her skull to remove her defiant eyes myself. So real that I could almost feel the warmth of her flesh on my fingers and hear her scream of agony. Shaking the thought away, I took a deep breath and swallowed back the anger rising in me, not wanting to lose control in front of my followers. I shrugged my shoulders as casually as I could.

"As you wish. You were born a whore, and that's what I shall call you. Listen now, bitch. Either you worship me like the God that I am, or you die. It's your choice, but you will be my slave anyway."

I gritted the words through my teeth with more anger than I wanted to show. If I were to be a God, I couldn't show weaknesses. I didn't want to appear weak before my worshippers, but that woman was pissing me off. Self-control wasn't one of my strong points; she would pay the price if she pushed me over the edge.

The woman spat back, "I will never join you! The Moon Goddess will get you for this! I…"

There was no use in listening to her anymore. She had made her choice. I concentrated on her, leaching her life force, feeling the strength of her wolf as I drank her soul. So that's where her fury came from; she wasn't human. I closed my eyes momentarily, enjoying the blissful feeling of replenishment. I couldn't hold a moan when her wolf's senses mixed with mine for a split second, filling me with a wild sensation and a primal need to fuck her mate. It was so strong that I got hard at the thought alone. The thought occurred to me that she might have been in heat. No wonder those fuckers were so attached to one another all the time.

My lip curved as I watched the woman fall lifeless to the floor. Everyone was still staring in silence. It was time for me to give them a show they wouldn't forget.

I channeled my energy into the woman's corpse, reanimating her body. She slowly rose back up, staring at me with that distinctive void look on her face. I grinned and asked Judah, "Untie her."

He nodded and executed what I asked. I ordered the woman, "Down on your knees."

The zombie did as she was told.

"Good, now come and kiss my hand."

I knew damn well how the woman would have been pissed if she could see this. I wished she could somehow see, but I knew she couldn't. I waited patiently as the reanimated corpse slowly walked on her knees up to me and kissed my hand. I slapped her face, pushed her back down after she righted herself, and then yelled at everyone.

"Now you see! Serve me! Or die and serve me as a zombie! The choice is simple. You will end up serving me either way."

The tied man and woman shivered in fear at my words. My worshippers put a hand on their chest, bowing their heads lowly.

Judah solemnly said, "We will always follow you, Harvester of death."

I waited to see if anyone dared to defy me, but everyone kept their heads down in approbation. I turned to the tied man and woman.

"What will you choose?"

They looked at me. The sweet look of defeat in their eyes mixed with resignation. Two things I loved seeing in my worshippers.

"I… I will serve you, Harvester of death," answered the man.

My eyes fell on the woman. She nodded nervously, tears falling down her cheeks.

"I will… follow too," she whispered, barely audible.

I spoke in a loud voice, "Rejoice yourself! Our family grows once more. Untie them!" I ordered my worshippers before adding, "Show them how it works around here."

Judah and a few other worshippers nodded.

"About her," I said, pointing to the zombie woman that had defied me when she was alive. "Make sure that her second life is a living hell."

I didn't think the zombies could have feelings, and they didn't need to feed, but I wanted her to suffer as much as possible just in case they could.

"Yes! Oh, Harvester of death!"

I walked back to my chambers, tired but happy with how things ended. All I needed now was to grow my army even more. Soon, I'd be ready to assert my vengeance.

Chapter 4 (Matthew)

Molly

I woke up holding Kelly in my arms. The past few weeks have been amazing. Since the pack decided to leave our job as guardians, my life had been entirely different. Suddenly, my fate wasn't chosen for me. The mark I was born with, the one bore by the chosen ones, was now nothing but a birthmark. I was thrilled that it didn't hold a particular meaning anymore. I could make plans for my future. Kelly and I have been talking about settling together when the pack moves. I've even thought about sealing the bond with her. Although I haven't spoken to her about it, my wolf has grown fond of hers. I only hoped she would accept.

Kelly stirred in her sleep. I enjoyed watching her sleeping. She was so beautiful. I had become attached to her. Being together made me realize how much I cared for her. I was now the next in line to become an Alpha since I was older than Bryan and wasn't destined to be sacrificed anymore. I couldn't help but think that Kelly would make an excellent Luna.

She had a sexy smirk when she opened her eyes, making her irresistible. I loved that look of hers. I smirked at the thought of what was going on in her mind, my cock twitching in anticipation. I wasn't expecting this, but I would gladly oblige. Her lips were on mine the minute she woke up, her hand going directly down to my morning erection. I moaned as she worked me in the ways she knew I liked. I grabbed her naked ass, squeezing her deliciously hard bun. She moaned when I glided a finger into her opening, realizing she was already dripping wet for me.

"Damn, girl. Have you been dreaming of naughty things? Already so wet!"

The way her lip curved upward was all I needed for an answer. I circled on her clit. "Such a naughty girl!"

She couldn't answer, moaning and writhing under my touch. Such a good girl! I couldn't wait to ravish her the way she liked it so much. I grunted as her hand kept stroking me hard.

"Matt, please!" she asked.

I whispered in her ear, her hard nipples brushing against me as I got closer, "Come for me, beautiful."

She bucked her back as I kept circling on her clit. Soon her legs shook as she cried my name. I slowed down my touches, my tongue dancing with hers.

Her eyes were still glassy from pleasure when I whispered in her ear, "Such a good girl."

I didn't wait for an answer, my cock rock hard for her. I entered her wet cunt, making her gasp. I could still feel her pulsing from her earlier climax. She felt like paradise. I adjusted to her cries, her moans being my reward. I kept thrusting into her, her pussy tightening around my cock. My wolf was fighting to get out. He wanted to make her ours. But I kept him in check; I needed to ask her before I sealed the bond.

Kelly dug her nails into my back, screaming my name. I couldn't hold back when I felt her come for a second time. I joined my moans to hers as I came hard, pleasure washing over me. I slowed my thrusts, letting her get down from her high. I lay beside her, wrapping my arms around her as I rested.

Kelly smiled as she kissed me.

"Good morning, Matt."

Her voice was honeyed, still filled with pleasure as she spoke. I kissed her back.

"Good morning, sweetheart. That's one way to wake up." I winked at her. She giggled at my comment.

"But you love it."

She nibbled my lower lip.

"Hm… As much as I love you."

"You love me?"

I chuckled. "I thought it was obvious."

She breathed in slowly. "I love you too, Matthew."

To hear her say it felt like the greatest gift. I hugged her tight, kissing every inch of her skin. I still couldn't believe how much my life had changed in the past few weeks. I was the luckiest wolf in the world.

We exited after a quick shower. Kelly looked beautiful in her light blue dress. I wanted to visit my father to see how the preparations for the pack's move were going. The faster we'd leave this place, the better I'd feel. It would be a new start, like a second coming to life, and I couldn't wait for it.

As we walked in the street, the rescue fairy team flew over our heads. They were the fairies the witches had mandated to look for missing people. There have been a few cases of missing people lately. The pack was growing wary, people didn't walk alone anymore, and the streets were deserted at night. A curfew had been instituted by my father to make sure no one dared to get out after sunset.

The witches had decided to put together teams of fairies. They were resilient, and there were a lot of them. They were small and could easily search everywhere. The teams were relaying themselves day and night. However, no missing person has been found yet. This raised many questions, and I couldn't help but wonder if this flow of missing people was related to the fact the pack had decided to move. Was it the price to pay so my life wouldn't need to be sacrificed? I hoped not, but I couldn't help but feel guilty about it. Only more reason to move away from here and start a new pack elsewhere. I hoped my curse wouldn't follow me to the end of the world. Maybe once we moved, I wouldn't have to worry about the demon anymore.

A small hand pulled on my shirt.

"Have you seen mommy?"

I looked down to see a small girl. Her blonde hair was messy, and her gray eyes filled with worry. My heart sank at the thought her mom could be one of the additions to the missing people. I bent down to her level to talk to her.

"Hi, there. What's your name?"

"Molly."

"That's a nice name. How old are you, Molly?"

She raised four fingers proudly. "I'm that much!"

"Wow! You're a big girl!"

The grin on her face was priceless but was soon replaced by worry.

"Have you seen mommy?"

"When have you last seen her?"

"She kissed me goodnight yesterday, but was gone when I woke up."

"Did you ask your dad?" Kelly asked.

The little girl shook her head.

"Daddy disappeared a week ago. Mommy said we needed to stick together until he came back. But the man in the wall said daddy won't come back."

I wondered for a minute if I had heard her right. Maybe it was only her imagination. A way for the child to deal with the loss of her father.

"A man in your wall?" I repeated.

Molly nodded.

"He talks to me at night. Says I'm special. He's coming for me soon."

Molly's gray eyes looked haunted as she stared at the void in front of her. Softly, she mumbled, "Look. Another one's gone."

I stared in the direction she was pointing but didn't see anything. A knot formed in my stomach. I took a deep breath, shoving away the uneasy feeling creeping on me.

"Well, why don't you come with us? We'll go to the pack's house and see if we can find your mommy, okay?"

The little girl nodded and hugged me. Her eyes sparkled, and I could see my reflection in them. Right now, I was the most important person in her little world, igniting warmth in my heart. I needed to help that kid; I wouldn't let her down. Her hand squeezed my fingers as we walked toward the pack's house.

"What does your mommy look like?" Kelly asked.

"Well. She's tall, has blonde hair, is very nice, and makes the best cookies!"

Kelly giggled.

"Do you know her name?" I asked her.

She nodded. "Her name is Theresa. Oh, and she has a scar on her right cheek. In the form of the letter 'L.'"

Well, that should help us identify her. I thought to myself.

"A scar?" asked Kelly.

The little girl shrugged her shoulders.

"She told me once it was from a battle when she was a child, but I don't know the details."

We soon arrived at the pack's house. My father was there with Esme. A few people from the pack were there, and a few humans from neighboring towns too.

One of the humans turned our way when we entered the pack's house. He was tall and had black hair. His brown eyes stared deeply at Kelly. No words were said, but she was staring at him the same way. This could mean only one thing; my heart broke at this realization. I could almost feel the invisible bond pulling them together. The words she spoke to me earlier didn't matter anymore. And the plans for our future were broken. Everyone knows you cannot resist the bond when you meet your fated mate. My hopes were shattered, but I wouldn't allow my tears to flow. Finding your fated mate was a blessing, and I should rejoice for my friend. My feelings were secondary in that matter. I only hoped I'd be blessed with finding my fated mate, too… if I had one. Born to be sacrificed, had the Moon Goddess also blessed me with a fated mate?

People were agitated, and everyone was speaking at the same time. My father spoke loudly.

"Please, everyone. Calm down."

The room went silent.

"We can't ignore the disappearances anymore!" said a woman.

"Their numbers are increasing every day!" added another.

Reassuringly, Esme said, "The fairy rescue squads are searching night and day."

"But it's not enough!" shouted one of the humans. "People are disappearing in our towns as well."

My father gestured, and everyone stopped talking. Molly took a few steps forward just as he was about to speak.

She stared at my father with her big gray eyes, her high-pitched voice asking, "Have you seen my mommy?"

I had no idea how she managed to let go of my hand and go forward without me noticing. I rushed forward and grabbed her in my arms.

"Sorry, Father." Then I whispered to her, "You can't interrupt the Alpha."

My father smiled gently.

"Son, who might this little girl be?"

The heat rose to my cheek as everyone turned to stare at me. I wasn't used to having a kid with me and felt clumsy and out of place.

"I found her outside. Her mom has been missing since last night, and her father for a week."

The room went silent. My father sighed heavily.

"Very well. It seems we must do more to settle this issue. We will organize a search party."

People cheered in the room, and Molly hugged me.

"Matthew, Kelly, you will lead the search party."

I nodded.

"Yes, Alpha," Kelly answered.

The man staring at Kelly earlier said, "I want to go too."

My father looked at him.

"Are you sure? This could be dangerous."

He nodded. Determination could be read in his eyes. I knew it wasn't only that. He wanted to be with his mate. It was only fair, and although it broke my heart, I would do the same if it was my fated mate.

"All right, then you will accompany them."

A hand rose from the people.

"Oh! Alpha! I want to go too."

We turned to see Gregory waving his hand. He might not have a wolf or magic, but he was always eager to help.

My father replied, "Gregory, three people is enough of a search party. This could be dangerous, and I don't want to risk too many lives."

A look of disappointment painted on Gregory's face, and I couldn't help but recall the other day when teenagers were making fun of him and saying how useless he was. I felt terrible for him. This was another rejection from the pack, and I didn't want him to feel this way.

"Father, please. I'm sure we can use Gregory's help."

My father had a surprised look on his face but nodded. I knew he would grant me this.

"Fine. You can go with them. But no one else."

"Oh, thank you," exclaimed Gregory.

"Everyone, dismiss," ordered my father.

People started to walk away, some lingering for a few minutes, talking together. I walked up to my father and Esme with Molly.

"Are you going to leave me?" asked Molly sadly.

I got down on my knee.

"Don't worry. I won't leave you alone. I'm going to go looking for your mommy, okay?"

She nodded happily. My father smiled at me.

"I never knew this fatherly side in you, Son."

I chuckled.

"I never knew it, either. Something lit inside me when she came to seek my help. I immediately felt a connection with Molly and a need to assist her."

He had an understanding look on his face.

I turned to Esme. "Can you please take care of her while I'm gone?"

The old witch smiled gently.

"Of course! She looks like she needs a bath too."

Molly giggled as she walked away happily with Esme. I was happy to see how easily the child trusted members of the pack.

"Matt…"

I could hear the worry in Kelly's voice when I turned around. I had never seen her eyes in dismay like that.

"What is it?"

She stared at me, searching for her words. My heart still ached, and my chest tightened. I knew what this was about. I swallowed the lump in my throat.

She whispered, "I have something I need to say."

I stopped her. I couldn't bear to hear it, yet it needed to be told.

"Don't. I already know. It's him, isn't it?"

She nodded, a single tear escaping her eye.

"How… How did you know?" Kelly asked, shocked.

"I saw how you two were looking at each other. I knew right away."

She grabbed my hand into hers, squeezing it.

"I'm so sorry, Matt. It doesn't change how I feel about you, but...."

I squeezed her hands back.

"That's okay. I understand. I'd do the same if I met my fated mate."

In her eyes, I could see how much she still cared about me and how much she didn't want to hurt me.

I smiled as best I could, considering how I felt. It was fake, but I didn't want her to feel bad about meeting her fated mate.

"It's okay, Kelly. You will always be my best friend."

I could see she was grateful for what I had said.

Someone cleared his throat behind us. I could guess without looking who it was. I smiled and let go of Kelly's hands. The man was staring intensely at us, his jaw clenched.

I spoke to him, "Hi. Sorry, I was just talking with my friend."

The man's expression softened, and he smiled, relieved.

"Nice to meet you. I'm Theo."

"Theo," Kelly repeated with a grin.

Theo and Kelly started to chat, both of them smiling. I could read the fire in Kelly's eyes. I didn't know if the human knew anything about fated mates, but I was sure that Kelly would teach him about it soon enough.

Watching them talk together was torturous. I wish I could have been given time to accept it was over between Kelly and me. My wolf was hurting, and I could only plaster a fake smile. I felt grateful that Gregory had volunteered to come with us. At least I wouldn't be alone with Kelly and Theo.

Gregory joined us, and we planned where we would start investigating.

Serena's POV

I was still shocked that our pack was moving. This was the place I was born and raised. It was strange to think that I wouldn't see this forest anymore. Where would we go? Would we be able to find a new place to live without fighting another pack? Werewolves were very territorial. I only hoped we wouldn't need to fight against them for stepping on their territory without knowing. More importantly, what would be the impact of leaving our job as keepers of Eurynomos's seal? That was the part that scared me the most. I didn't want Matthew to be sacrificed. I didn't want anyone to be sacrificed anymore. But what if the demon was to be set free? What chance did we stand against a demon? Bile rose in my mouth at this thought.

Ancient texts spoke of a time when Eurynomos reigned freely over the world of the living, killing, and feeding of his victims. He loved flesh and didn't care for anyone. He spread fear worldwide, leaving rivers of blood and carnage wherever he went. It lasted for centuries; people kept their doors and windows locked. The children hid at night as Eurynomos seemed to love the shadows. Only the Moon Goddess could stop him and seal him in this sepulcher. I was forever grateful to her, and my magic was a daily reminder of the gift and the task she had given to my people. Her gift was indeed cursed. With our mission came the burden of sacrificing someone. I couldn't help but feel guilty at the thought of betraying her.

But the pack had spoken. I was part of the pack, and I needed to act accordingly. I would follow the Alpha's orders. His and Esme's orders. I only hoped we wouldn't doom ourselves.

When I got to Esme's house, a little girl was playing in her garden. She looked like a doll with her white skin and two long ponytails of golden hair. I stared for a moment, mesmerized by her lullaby. Butterflies flew around the girl as she sang in the flower field.

"... for rain has a little silver dew and trees arbor all fruits. All your fears will vanish. Forget your worries, and follow me."

These lyrics sounded quite peculiar, especially for a girl her age. She finally noticed me and stopped singing.

I smiled at her. "That was a nice song!"

She grinned. "Thanks! I was signing it for the lady."

I looked around but couldn't see anyone.

"What lady?"

The girl pointed beside her.

"She was right there, but she's gone now."

I wondered for a moment if I had been so concentrated on the little girl that I missed someone standing beside her. At this moment, Esme got out of her house.

"Serena! I see you've met Molly."

I nodded. "I sure did! I didn't know you had a friend with you."

"Well, it's more like Matthew's."

I frowned.

"Matthew doesn't have a child, does he?"

Esme burst out laughing.

"Dear God, no! But he found her and went to search for her missing parents."

My eyes fell on the little girl playing innocently in the flowers. To have her parents missing must be taking quite a toll on her. The poor child.

"Well, nice to meet you, little miss."

Molly got up and hugged me.

"I like you."

Her little arms squeezed me tight, and I couldn't do anything but squeeze her back.

Esme asked the child, "Would you like a cookie while I talk with Serena?"

Molly nodded and ran inside Esme's house.

"She's quite special, isn't she?" Esme commented.

I nodded. "I noticed."

Esme continued, "I can't put my finger on it. She's not a witch nor a werewolf. She's not quite human, either. I feel something pure in her, but I'm unsure what it is."

"Huh, that does raise a lot of questions!"

"Yes, but don't worry, my dear. I'll figure it out."

"Of course! If someone can figure it out, it's you!"

I had faith in Esme; she was the oldest and wisest of the pack. Nothing could stay a mystery from her for a long time.

We entered the house. Molly was already sitting at the table, her legs swinging happily, waiting for her cookie. Esme grabbed a cookie from the jar while talking.

"Serena, I need you to check on the sepulcher's seal. We need to know if it has started to weaken. We must leave before the seals break."

That dreaded moment when the seal falters. The moment the sacrifice is necessary. My heart raced for a moment.

"What will we do if it's already weakened?"

Esme frowned. "Please, Serena. Let's worry about that only if it happens. I think the seal is still intact, but I must be sure. And I can't go and check myself."

Right. She had to take care of Molly and of… "How is Odilia doing?"

"She's okay but still weak. She's resting. I'm still waiting for news of her husband."

I nodded. "I'm glad to know she's okay."

Esme pinched her lips.

"Still, as I told you, I suspect her husband is a werewolf. Her pregnancy is not that of a normal human, and I will need to eventually talk to her about it."

I nodded. This news will shock her, but hopefully, she'll be able to accept this new information as smoothly as she took in our pack when she first arrived here.

"Please. I would like to be here when you tell her."

Esme nodded. "Yes, of course. Anyway, I need to be sure her husband is a werewolf before telling her about it. I can't afford to be mistaken. She agreed to let me draw some blood from her. I started to decant a purification potion on the blood extract. It should take a few hours, but I should know if my theory is true by then."

Once again, I was amazed by Esme's knowledge.

"Right, then I'll go check on the seal right away. I want to see the results of this potion when I get back."

Esme nodded and said goodbye as I took my leave.

Chapter 5 (Serena)

The seal

Eurynomos's sepulcher wasn't far East from the pack, but no one ventured there. The place was desolated, and an eerie silence filled the air as I climbed the granite stairs. I couldn't get over how beautiful this place was every time I visited. Decorated with intricate patterns and sculptures hanging from the ceiling, all in richness and marvel. One could have believed that a queen lived here, so much the place exuded opulence and detail. It was a pity that this place was the holding place of a demon.

As I reached the top of the stairs, I stared at the gray clouds filling the sky, the sun rays giving them an orange tint. A permanent fog seemed to surround this place as if sealing it from the rays of light. Everything was as when I came last time. In front of the stairs stood an imposing statue of the Goddess. Her ever-watching eyes stared at me. I held my breath, afraid she could see me through the statue's eyes and know we intended to betray her.

Beyond the statue stood the main building with its imposing dome ceiling, taller than everything else.

I pushed through the imposing doors and made my way inside. A subdued light filtered through the windows. Speckles of dust floated in the air as if held in place by some magic. Time didn't seem to flow the same way inside the sepulcher, and it always gave me an uncanny feeling. The sooner I'd be done here, the better I'd feel.

My footsteps echoed around me as I walked through the corridor. I glanced at the cracks in the ceiling. A vestige of past attacks. A time when some zealous people tried to break in to free the demon. I didn't know who in their right mind could want to unleash a demon from its prison, but my ancestors had to fight the trespassers back, leaving permanent damage to the ceiling, a reminder that it was necessary to have people guarding this place. Since the attack, the ceremonial scepter has been kept in the pack's house. It was thought it'd be better if the scepter necessary to release Eurynomos's seal was not kept inside the sepulcher. This way, if someone was to break in, they wouldn't have the tool needed to open the seal. That goes without saying that the scepter holds great power. In the wrong hands, it could summon havoc to this world.

I finally arrived at the vast, round sacrificial room. At the center of it stood an altar. Bile rose into my mouth at the sight of the blood-stained floor around the altar. A sense of relief washed over me, knowing no innocent blood would ever be spilled in this place. I quickly paced to the seal. Only witches could perform the task of checking the seal, as it required a powerful spell.

Concentrating, I channeled the required spell. The magic started pouring into me through my soul. Filled with this power, my vision shifted, strings of energy appeared where there were none just seconds before. As faint as it was, the sun shone brightly through the darkness, each ray caressing the veil of emptiness, leading spirits away. The demon's seal became visible, glowing intensely in blue. Reassured, I was about to break the spell when I noticed something unusual. The green flow of the life force seemed weaker than usual. Usually, it poured like a mighty torrent, but there was only a small gully that flowed gently. I didn't know what this meant, but it couldn't be good. I cut the spell and hurried back to the pack.

Tarriel was whispering to Esme when I got to her house. They turned to look at me when I got there. I could hear Odilia talking with Molly in a room further.

Esme looked at me worryingly. "So, how is the seal?"

I got closer to them, so I could whisper.

"The seal is good. It hasn't weakened yet."

She let out a sigh of relief.

"At least that's one good news."

I bit my lip nervously.

"Well… There's this thing, though. The life force usually flows strongly. But when I looked, it was only a small, weak strand flowing."

Esme's eyes filled with fear at my words.

"By the Moon Goddess's grace! This can't be good."

I nodded. "I know, but I have no idea what it means."

She took a deep breath. "Let's just hope we find out sooner than later what's happening."

Tarriel stood there, listening to us. I asked him, "Any news of Gerald?"

He winced. "That's what I was discussing before you arrived. I found Gerald in the forest. He was walking weirdly, limping on his leg. I tried getting to him but saw many people with him too."

He paused, staring in front of him as if seeing the images as he was telling them.

"That's when I realized some of them had deep gashes and wounds. They looked like they should have been dead. But somehow, they were walking. I heard a few of them grunt, but none looked like they could speak. This isn't normal."

A shiver ran down my back as I listened with fright to Tarriel's story. This was worrisome. I had never heard of anything similar in the past.

"What are you saying?" I asked anxiously.

He came inches from my face, his hands firmly on my shoulders. He spoke every word calmly but resolutely, "I'm telling you, the dead are walking."

"That can't be true!" I shook myself free from his grip.

"Serena! I saw them with my own eyes! Would I lie to you?"

My chin trembled as I stared at him, a sudden numbness filling me. I had known him for so long; I knew he was telling the truth. His deep brown eyes were piercing me, waiting for an answer.

I mumbled, "No. You wouldn't lie to me."

Pain shot through my chest at that moment, and tears threatened to fall from my eyes. It was the scariest thing I had ever heard, and I was afraid for my life and everyone's life!

Tarriel's strong arms wrapped around me. I let him cradle me in his body's warmth and masculine scent until I calmed down and could think straight again.

"Do you think it could be related to the flow of the life force?" I asked faintly.

Tarriel answered nothing, but Esme's eyes widened, "Maybe…."

A chill ran done my spine.

Esme said aloud, "People are disappearing, and the dead are rising. What dark magic is causing this?"

Tarriel shrugged his shoulders. He spoke softly, his deep voice resonating through his chest, "I don't know, but I think it'd be best we don't tell Odilia her husband is undead."

I was speechless at the realization. Of course, we couldn't tell her that. Esme nodded and added, "Yes, but we must speak to her. She needs to be bitten by a werewolf, and soon."

I gasped, my heart racing.

"Does that mean you confirmed that…"

Esme got a vial from a container. It contained a white residue. I watched closely as Esme explained,

"Yes!" answered Esme. "The white powder reacted to the wolf's genes. Odilia's baby's father was a werewolf."

Tarriel's eyes widened.

"I've always thought Gerald was a great hunter. I guess it was because of his wolf."

This raised many questions. "Wouldn't Odilia know if he was a werewolf? She would have met his wolf already?"

Tarriel pondered. "Maybe he couldn't change into his wolf form?"

I exclaimed, "These cases are very rare! There had been a few occurrences in the past, but… Only a few people have had this problem."

"But it could explain how his wife was unaware that her husband was a werewolf," argued Tarriel.

Esme nodded. "Anyhow, Odilia's body won't be able to adapt to the fast-growing rhythm of the baby. She needs to be bitten for her body to adapt."

Tarriel exclaimed, "By the Moon Goddess! This will be a lot for her to take in."

I knew he was right, but I wondered if there was any easy way to tell Odilia. The death of her husband and the fact he was a werewolf. And now she needed to be bitten by one to survive her pregnancy. Let alone the fact that being bitten by a werewolf meant it sealed her destiny to a man she didn't know.

Esme pinched her lips. "I'm afraid we don't have much time. She's growing weaker by the hour. She will need to be strong."

I closed my eyes, taking a deep breath.

"Okay, let me tell her, then."

They both stared at me. I continued, "I'm the one who brought her here. I'm the one who told her about werewolves and magic."

They nodded, but Esme replied, "Okay, but I will be there if she needs support."

Tarriel nodded, too. "So will I."

I braced myself. "Hopefully, the beginning of my friendship with her will soften the news."

Esme raised her hands to the ceiling. "Let's pray to the Moon Goddess that you're right."

We made our way to Odilia's room. A knot formed in my stomach. This moment wouldn't be easy, but it was necessary.

Matthew's POV

We were walking north. I walked in front with Gregory while Kelly and Theo stayed behind us. I didn't want to eavesdrop, but I could hear them talking, and it was tearing my heart out. Although I was happy for Kelly. I kept reminding myself that finding your fated mate was a blessing. I would have done the same thing! I couldn't help but feel this tightening in my chest. I think I had really fallen in love with her. Whom was I kidding? I even had planned to ask her to bond with me, for God's sake! Of course, I had fallen in love with her!

For a second, I had forgotten about fated mates. I thought I could live happily with her. I let myself have dreams and open my heart for the first time, only to have it crushed. I was a fool. But I couldn't be mad with Kelly. I would have done the same thing if I had met my fated mate. It would hurt and take some time, but I'd get over it.

Of course, seeing them both smiling and talking wasn't making it easier. I sucked in a breath. I was stronger than this. I was the Alpha's son, next in line to lead the pack. Born on a blessed night, and now free of my curse. I had been given a second chance at life. I wouldn't waste my time moping around forever.

"Thanks for taking me with you."

Gregory was grinning happily. I smiled back at him.

"Of course! All help is welcome!"

"Well, not everyone in the pack thinks I can help. I'm glad to be part of a group, for once."

My wolf was growing annoyed. He was mad at the pack members for treating Gregory this way. As the future Alpha, he wanted to protect everyone, and I agreed.

I clenched my jaw. "No one should be treating you that way. You're as important as everyone else in the pack."

He seemed grateful for my words. "Thanks, no one ever said something like that to me."

He stopped briefly, staring weirdly at the void in front of him. I called up to him, "Gregory?" But he didn't react.

Kelly and Theo caught up to us.

"What's going on?" asked Kelly.

I shrugged my shoulders and pointed to Gregory. We all watched as he looked at the sky and turned his head in every way. I wasn't sure what was going on. I knew he had no wolf, so he couldn't be sniffing the air. I would have caught the scent before him, if anything. He then suddenly looked back at us as if remembering something.

"We need to head southwest!"

We all looked at him weirdly.

"Are you sure? We had decided to go north earlier."

He spoke passionately, "I know! But I have this gut feeling. We need to walk southwest."

I had my doubts. We had decided to go north since the human town with missing people was that way. It seemed logical that whatever made people disappear must have been between our pack and their cities.

He continued, "Please! Trust me on this one!"

He seemed so confident, and I knew he wanted to help as much as possible. I figured, in the end, there was no harm in trying Gregory's suggestion. We could always turn back if there was nothing, and it would be nice for Gregory to feel he was leading the way.

I smiled at him. "Okay, we'll follow your hunch."

Kelly looked surprised, but I knew she wouldn't question my decision. Theo shrugged his shoulders; he would follow Kelly anywhere she went. He might have been human; the mate bond was pulling on him. Gregory grinned as we started walking southwest.

We walked for a while, going further down south than I had ever gone. The forest was beautiful, and I let Gregory lead the walk. I could feel a new sense of belonging to something emanating from him. I was happy for him. After all, isn't that what we all want? To be a part of something bigger, to have a connection, and to help?

The more we walked, the more my wolf was getting restless. I could smell a faint scent in the air that I couldn't grasp. It smelled like lilac flowers, but I knew there weren't any around here, and they didn't bloom this time of year. Somehow I felt drawn to this scent. The stronger it got, the harder my wolf fought for control.

A faint voice reached my ears, "Help! Please help!"

All hell went loose. There was no holding him back now, not that I wanted to. I embraced the change and started running as fast as possible from where the scent came from. I could hear Kelly calling after me, but I didn't care. She needed help. She needed me. One word resonated through my mind as I ran with all my might, "Mate."

Chapter 6 (Elisen)

Soul Nymph

My eyelids felt heavy as I fought to open them. How many times have I slipped unconscious? I've lost count. What day was it? If I didn't die from the beating of those thugs, I would surely die of thirst and hunger. The ropes that tied me to the big tree were the only thing holding me up, as I didn't have the strength to stand alone. I barely felt my fingers as they had been tied over my head for such a long time now that I wondered if blood still ran through them.

There they were, discussing how they'll torture me next. I tried telling them so many times that I wasn't responsible for the missing people. But they didn't believe me. They wanted to blame someone, and I stumbled on their path. Suddenly, one of them looked my way and sneered when he saw I was awake.

Breathing hurt, and I shivered from fear. I didn't want to know what they planned to do to me next. Gathering the little strength I had left, I tried once again as loudly as I could, hoping this time someone heard me.

"Help! Please help!"

My voice was not as strong as I wished it was. The man I've come to know as Fred had an evil smirk on his face.

"How many times have I told you, bitch? It's no use crying for help. No one will come for you."

I swallowed in fear as he came toward me. A spark of pleasure filled his eyes at the thought of what he would do to me. I shut my eyes closed, bracing for the pain. The contact of his fist on my jaw made my head turn to the left, warm blood dripping from my mouth. Bile rose to my mouth, but I swallowed it, not wanting to throw up.

"Come on, bitch! Open your eyes. It's funnier this way."

I kept my eyes closed, too weak to open them. Fred snarled, and the other men joined him.

"You know what will happen to you if you don't open them."

A shiver ran down my back. Gathering whatever strength I had left, I opened my eyes. The evil smile on Fred's face made my blood run cold. God only knew what evil he had planned to do to me next.

A sudden growl filled the air.

"What the fuck?" Fred asked.

All the men turned their heads to stare at something behind me, but I couldn't look as I was tied. One of the men started to run, but the others stayed, preparing their knives.

Suddenly, a huge brown wolf jumped on one of the men. The wolf swiftly bit the neck of the man, ripping his flesh out, blood gushing to the ground, the sound of the man's screams filling the air. I wrinkled my nose at the metallic smell of blood but could do nothing more. I didn't know where the wolf came from, but I was glad he was there. Fred lunged at the wolf, digging his knife into his back, but the wolf was unimpressed. The wolf turned his head toward me, staring at me for a split second. His eyes shimmered with something I couldn't quite understand and seemed to stare at my soul. He turned his attention back to Fred, leaving me to wonder if I had imagined this.

With one bite, he got Fred to release the knife. The other men cursed, and one of them yelled, "What the fuck? I'm not staying here!"

He started running, but the others watched warily, unsure if they should attack. Raising himself on his legs, he was almost as tall as Fred. The wolf pushed Fred to the ground, pushing his front paws on the man with all his weight. He cursed as the wolf's teeth were dangerously close to his face.

"What are you fuckfaces waiting for? Attack the damn beast already!"

The wolf snarled at them, and two other men ran away. I rejoiced at the sight of my attackers fleeing, wondering how to untie myself once they were dealt with. Fred's screams got me out of my thoughts. The wolf was scratching and biting him. Blood was everywhere, and I couldn't distinguish most of his face already. The other men were nowhere to be seen. I guess they fled when I wasn't looking.

I stared at the wolf as he gave Fred what he deserved. I thought for a moment that maybe I should have been scared of what the wolf would do once he was done dealing with him, but somehow, I knew he wouldn't hurt me.

"Matt!" a woman's voice shouted from behind me.

Soon, a woman and two men came running from behind me and surrounded the wolf.

"Matt! What are you doing?" asked the first man.

"You shouldn't have run like that! You should have waited for us!" scolded the woman.

Were they talking to the wolf? Fred wasn't moving anymore, and the wolf stopped attacking, satisfied. He stared at me, his fur stained with blood. They all turned and noticed me for the first time.

"Oh my gosh!" the woman exclaimed, covering her mouth.

I had no idea who they were, but they were definitely with the wolf, so I figured they weren't a threat. Not like I could have fought back anyway.

"Let's get her untied," the other man said.

My arms fell down when he cut the ropes holding them up. My head felt dizzy, and I felt a sudden warmth filling me. Black spots blurred my vision before darkness engulfed me.

I was being transported; everything was still black.

"Careful," said a man's voice.

My head was spinning as I fell back unconscious.

I wanted to open my eyes so badly, but I couldn't. The world was still moving around me.

"We need to get her warmed up," said a woman.

"Lay her there," suggested a man.

"I'm keeping her in my arms," growled another man.

"But Matt!" interjected the woman.

I fell back into darkness.

When I woke up the next time, I wasn't being moved around anymore. I kept my eyes closed, listening to sounds around me, taking in my surroundings. I could hear the crackle of a fire. I felt strong arms holding me as I lay on someone's lap, his body's heat surrounding me. An enticing scent of spice emanated from him, filling my mind. All I could think of was that I'd love to drown myself in his arms.

I didn't dare to look yet. I basked in his warmth, listening.

"Do you think she'll wake up?" whispered a woman.

"I don't know what I'll do if she doesn't," the deep voice of the man holding me resonated through his chest right to my heart. It was filled with worry, and he squeezed me while speaking.

"I'm sure she'll wake up," spoke the woman.

"Yes, don't lose hope," said a man.

The man holding me sighed.

"Come on, eat," said another man.

"Only if I'm able to eat while holding her."

The man holding me softly moved one of his arms to grab something to eat. Still, he held me tight with his other arm. I could hear the other men and the woman talking a little further.

The thought of food was driving me mad as much as the curiosity to look at the man holding me. I felt drawn to him without having met him. I had never felt something like this before. It was irrational. Staying silent, I opened my eyes.

His hair was brown, and his torso, or what I could see of it, looked broad and muscular. A bowl was placed on the ground beside him. He was eating while taking care not to disturb me. The way he cared for me made me feel special. I wondered why he was so nice to me. Was he feeling the same way as I was about him? His blue eyes fell on me, and he grinned.

"You're awake!" he whispered in relief.

Everyone stopped talking. The weight of their stare made me shy. I nodded.

He asked gently, "Can you talk?"

"Yes," I replied, my voice sounding hoarser than intended.

"Let's get you some water. It should help."

I was still feeling feeble. It seemed like forever since I had drunk water. My lips were chapped, and this would surely help my sore throat. Gently, he helped me sit, his arm wrapping around me. I rested my back against his chest, sitting on his lap. My head was still spinning. With his free hand, he brought a mug of water to me, making me drink. Each sip invigorated me, my body having been deprived of it for so long that I felt alive again. His strong hand covered mine, and he slowly straightened the cup.

"Slow down. You can't drink too fast, or you'll be sick."

I knew he was right, and I couldn't do anything but nod.

"How are you feeling?" he asked gently.

I took a moment to think about it. Strangely, my wounds didn't seem to hurt, and I wondered how it was possible. With how those thugs treated me, I expected to be in pain.

"Weak, but good, actually. I'm not hurting," I answered, still puzzled.

He smiled as he answered, "I'm glad it worked."

"What worked?"

"I gave you a few drops of my blood," he explained.

I stared at him in shock. "You did what?"

Fear flashed in his eyes for a moment. "Please don't be mad. You were dying. I had to save you."

"How did giving me drops of your blood save me?"

"Don't you know what I am?"

I drowned myself in his blue eyes. I couldn't help but wonder what he meant.

"You're human, aren't you?"

His lips curved up in the sexiest way.

"I'm a werewolf. My blood has healing power."

His words shocked me. I had never heard about werewolves. But now that I thought about earlier, the wolf saving me was him. A small purr escaped his chest. It was unexpected but comforting at the same time.

I hesitated but had to know. "Will I… become like you?"

He chuckled at my question.

"Because you drank my blood?"

I nodded slowly.

He shook his head. "No. It doesn't work that way. You need to be born a werewolf." He paused, then added, "You're not too scared, are you?"

I shook my head. I already knew the answer, but I asked anyway, "You're the one who saved me?"

He nodded, and I smiled, giving warmth to my cheeks. "Thank you for saving me!"

"I heard you cry for help," he explained.

A throat cleared itself.

"Would you introduce your girlfriend to us?" teased the woman.

A soft growl escaped the man's chest.

"Don't say stupid things. She just woke up."

I looked at the woman. She extended her hand, smiling friendly.

"Hi, I'm Kelly. Nice to meet you!"

I grabbed her hand weakly.

"Thanks for saving me. All of you. I'm Elisen."

"Elisen," the man holding me answered with a deep, husky voice. Hearing my name on his lips sounded like it was meant to be.

"I'm Matthew," he added. His name resonated right to my soul. Somehow, it's like I knew him for lifetimes.

One of the men said, "I'm Gregory."

Then the other one added, "And I'm Theo."

Watching the group that saved me, I couldn't help but be grateful. If they had not crossed my path and Matthew had not heard my cry for help, I would surely be dead.

"Nice to meet you all."

"I have so many things to ask you," whispered Matthew, the hot air from his breath rolling on my skin, giving me shivers.

"Yes, we all do," added Kelly.

"I want to get to know you too. But do you think I could get something to eat first?"

I didn't want to break this conversation, but my need to eat was getting too urgent. My stomach hurt from hunger.

"Of course!" exclaimed Kelly, who hurried to fetch me a bowl of stew. "How long was it since you ate?"

I honestly had no idea how long it had been. My memory of the last few days was too fuzzy.

"I don't know. I've been tied and tortured by those thugs for a few days."

A growl escaped Matt's chest, and he tightened his hold on me protectively. His words were gentle when he spoke, "No wonder you passed out. Eat, we'll talk after."

I grabbed the bowl, but it felt heavy, and my arms shook. Matthew was staring at me, waiting for me to eat. My arms felt like they could give out. I felt embarrassed to be in such a state.

He grabbed the bowl from me, whispering, "Let me help you."

I felt grateful that his voice didn't hold judgment. He grabbed the pieces of food and fed me one spoonful at a time. Although it was weird to be fed by someone, I had to admit that my body wasn't fully healed yet.

I whispered, "You don't need to do this."

He shook his head. "I need to. You're too weak to eat by yourself."

His eyes held untold words. I murmured, "But you barely know me."

He disagreed once again, "Nonsense! You're my mate."

I frowned. "Mate?"

He nodded. "The Moon Goddess blesses us with one mate. Someone to love and cherish forever. Perfect for us in any way. Made especially for us, as we are made for them. Can't you feel it?"

His words didn't make sense, but my heart knew they were true, even though I barely knew him. The thought of having someone fated to love was beautiful, and I wanted to think it was true. I nodded. "I do feel it."

His face lit up with the most beautiful smile, melting my heart. His fingers brushed my cheek gently as he added, "It's normal for me to take care of you. That's what mates do."

He kept feeding me as questions filled my mind. I was ready to accept the idea of fated mates but also confused. He must have felt it since he asked, "What is it?"

Everyone was looking at us, but there was no reason to keep this a secret.

"Do you know what I am?"

They all shook their heads. Kelly said gently, "We were wondering but didn't dare to ask."

Matthew spoke in a husky voice, "Your light purplish skin shimmers under the stars in the most beautiful ways. You don't have the elves' pointy ears. Your emerald eyes glimmer with an unknown force, and your dark purple hair twirls in ways that I want to lose my fingers into them."

His words stole my breath away. Never had anyone said anything like this to me. The people I usually met didn't care about my feelings and were either rude or would stare until I felt uncomfortable. I smiled at their words.

"I'm a soul nymph."

They all watched me in wonder, unsure of what this meant.

"A soul nymph?" asked Matthew, softly caressing my arm.

"I'm not surprised you haven't heard of us. As you see, we guide the departed souls to the afterlife. We execute the Gods judgment on the departed. The good ones are directed to the Elysian Plains and the bad ones to the Underworld. Soul nymphs usually stay away from the living."

Matthew softly said, "I'm glad you ventured here, or I would have never met you. But I can feel something bothering you. What is it?"

I let out a long breath, staring into his beautiful blue eyes. They were as deep as the sea and held me spellbound.

"Soul nymphs don't usually have feelings. We are a pure race devoted to the Gods. Love is a foreign concept to me, although I have heard of it. Soul nymphs don't reproduce; we are born from the soul realm at the Gods' will."

Worry filled Matthew's eyes, and for a moment, I feared he might crumble into pieces. I quickly added, "I do have these feelings for you. I can feel this attraction. I can't deny that this fated mate story of yours seems to be the source of it." I thought for a moment as I couldn't find the right words. "It's just all so new to me."

Matthew held out a breath of relief and smiled.

"Well, then. Let me teach you everything about love."

His lips crushed on mine the next instant, my heartbeat increasing, and my heart filling with this warm, pleasant feeling. I closed my eyes, enjoying this delightful moment, as Matthew's fingers lost themselves in my hair, his tongue twirling with mine. Surrounded by his scent and warmth, I finally understood why people valued love as much as they did.

I opened my eyes when Matthew backed away.

He was grinning. "So, what do you think?"

I also grinned, my eyes staring into his, sharing a secret link only our souls could understand.

"Astounding!" was the only thing I could answer.

Matthew smirked, and I knew then that I could never live without him again. I was eager to learn everything I could about love, and I would let him be my teacher.

Kelly asked, "You said your kind usually stays away from us. So, what were you doing out here?"

I nodded. "Something is disturbing the flow of souls."

They all stared at me with questioning looks.

"My clan has sent me to find out what's preventing the souls from going to the afterlife. But as I was walking, I got caught by those thugs. They took my swords away, tied and tortured me, and you found me."

Theo searched in his backpack.

"Are those your swords?"

He got my two swords out of his bag.

"Yes, they are!"

He handed them to me.

"We found them after killing the thugs. I thought they looked nice. I'd never seen such a metal, so I took them with me."

"Yes, they are made of a soul-severing metal forged by the demigods."

"Why would you need soul-severing swords?" asked Theo.

I snickered. "You'd be surprised what a damned soul will do to avoid going to the Underworld."

Matthew smirked. "Good thing you have the swords, then."

Kelly added, "Let's finish eating and set up a camp for the night."

Chapter 7 (Serena)

Be Prepared

We walked to Odilia's room. Molly was telling a story about fairies and flowers. The little girl stopped talking when we entered the room, her big gray eyes staring at us. Never had I seen such beautiful eyes. They were haunting as if they held the darkest mysteries. Yet, innocence shone through, the purity of a child.

"He doesn't like you," Molly stated when we entered the room.

I asked the girl, "Who doesn't like me?"

She shook her head, pointing to Esme. "Not you, her."

Esme frowned. "Whom are you talking about?"

The little girl answered naturally, "The man in the wall. He said you're meddling your nose where it doesn't belong. He said he'll set him free, whether you like it or not."

As I stood there, wondering whom Molly was talking about, Esme clenched her jaw.

"I don't care what this man in the wall thinks. I meddle my nose where it's necessary."

The little girl rose to her feet and hugged me before hugging Esme.

"I don't care what he thinks. I love you both."

I caressed the girl's head lovingly. We needed to talk with Odilia alone. I suggested, "Why don't you play in the flowers outside?"

Molly's face lightened up.

"Can a fairy join me?"

I looked at Esme, who explained, "I called fairies to keep her company the other day. I think she appreciated it."

Molly grinned. "Yes! They're so beautiful and nice!"

I smiled and summoned two fairies to join us. One landed in the girl's hand, and she gently ran her finger over the fairy's hair, the dust scattering in her hand. The little girl smiled widely.

"There, now go play with your little friends."

"Thank you!" the little girl shouted before running off to play with the fairies.

"That kid is special," mumbled Esme with her arms crossed. I understood what Esme meant by that. It was the second time I heard the girl talk about the man in the wall. I didn't know whom she was talking about, but it made me uneasy.

We waited to be sure Molly was away before talking to Odilia. When we were finally alone with her, she looked at us, breaking the silence, "I take it that for you three to be here, it probably isn't good news."

She was calm and had an understanding tone, but her eyes were full of worry. I took a deep breath.

I spoke calmly, "We found Gerald."

Odilia waited anxiously for me to finish talking, but I wasn't sure how to tell her. My mouth felt dry, and I only managed to whisper, "I'm sorry, Odilia."

Tears started to flow down her cheeks. She whispered, her lips trembling, "That's okay. I figured when he wasn't coming home that something was wrong."

I wrapped my arms around her, waiting for her cries to slow. I felt defenseless against this torrent of sadness. There was nothing I could do to mend her broken heart. When she finally calmed down, I wiped the tears from her face.

My chest tightened, and a lump filled my throat. I knew what I needed to tell her would only hurt her more.

I spoke calmly, "We found something else."

Odilia's green eyes stared deeply into mine.

"Is it a good or a bad thing?"

I bit my lip.

"Gerald was a werewolf."

Her eyes opened wide. "What? Are you sure? He never mentioned this."

I nodded. "We are."

Odilia frowned. "Shouldn't I have seen him change into a wolf? How can you be sure?"

"Remember when I did some blood tests?" asked Esme.

Odilia nodded. Esme continued, "We discovered your baby is a werewolf. Since you're human, it means the father was a werewolf."

I watched as the shock of the news hit her like a typhoon, destroying everything she knew about the man she loved.

As her world crumbled, Odilia put a hand over her mouth, her hands shaking. "Oh my gosh! Gerald never told me."

Tarriel said calmly, "We think maybe Gerald couldn't turn into a wolf."

Odilia asked in surprise, "Is that even a thing?"

Tarriel nodded. "Maybe he didn't even know himself. It can happen in rare cases. It's possible his parents never told him. Was he raised in a human town?"

Odilia's voice was shaking, "He grew up at the orphanage. He never knew his parents. That's why he was so eager to become a father."

Her voice broke, and she let out silent sobs.

Esme continued as gently as she could, "You're sick because the baby is a werewolf."

Odilia asked, "Aren't humans and werewolves compatible? I thought your pack consisted of werewolves and humans?"

Esme nodded. "Yes, but they form a bond before having a baby. You see, when the werewolf bites his lover, it seals a bond between them, but it also modifies the genes of the human to make her compatible with him."

"It modifies them genetically? They turn into a werewolf?"

Esme laughed. "No, nothing like that! It merely adjusts their body so that they can reproduce."

Silence fell in the room while we waited for Odilia to take in what we had told her. It was a lot to take in at once, and I wished we could give her more time to process everything. But time was against us. I knew Odilia was strong; she was already taking this easier than I thought she would. I was optimistic she'd be able to cope with this. And if not, we were there for her.

Odilia pondered briefly before asking, "What will happen to me? My baby is a werewolf, but I hadn't bonded with Gerald."

There wasn't an easy way to say it, so I just said, "If you don't bond with a werewolf very soon, you will die. Your body won't be able to cope with the baby's growth."

The news hit her like a dagger in the heart. I worried for a moment if she would make it through. That woman had just had her own life turned upside down. Emotions can do tricky things to the mind. I watched as Odilia crumbled into tears again. She held on to her belly; it was the only thing she had left. That same thing that could kill her if she didn't bond with a werewolf soon—the source of joy and hope, and also her sickness.

There was nothing I could do other than hug her and wait for her to calm down. It seemed like an eternity, but when she finally stopped crying, she asked, her voice barely audible, "What will I do? I don't want to die! Is there someone who can bond with me?"

Right on cue, Tarriel took a step forward.

"I will. I was Gerald's friend. It would be an honor to take care of his wife."

The way he said it might have sounded weird, but I knew he meant it in a friendly way. It also meant he was giving up on finding his fated mate. This was a big sacrifice. Tarriel was a good man, a strong warrior, and a good hunter. I knew he would take good care of Odilia.

Just then, a growl was heard from the window. A man stormed into the room, shouting, "Mine!"

Odilia screamed and grabbed Tarriel's arm. Precisely the opposite of what needed to be done to calm the man. I knew from how he was reacting that Odilia was his fated mate, whether she knew it or not.

Tarriel shouted to the man, "Calm down! I didn't know she was yours!"

But the man was filled with rage. He removed his t-shirt, showing his broad muscled chest, tying his blond hair back in a bun.

"Get your dirty hands off my mate!"

Tarriel got away from Odilia. The man was still unnerved, but he calmed himself when he saw that Tarriel was far from Odilia. It was a natural reaction for a werewolf, claiming what was rightfully his, given by the Moon Goddess.

"Garry, please, calm down. You don't want to frighten your mate!" ordered Esme.

Garry immediately stopped at those words and stared at Odilia, tenderness and passion showing through his eyes. The last thing he wanted to do was to scare Odilia. I knew he probably got caught in the thought of another wolf marking his mate.

"Sorry," he whispered.

Odilia was watching Garry, trembling. She had no idea the werewolf was her mate, the one made especially for her by the Moon Goddess. She didn't know his rage was due to seeing another man close to her. This was routine for us in the pack. But for someone outside the pack, this must have been very frightening, considering everything she had just gone through.

I approached Odilia, reassuring her. On the other side of the bed, Garry was studying me, staying close to his mate. He was watching Tarriel from a distance, making sure he didn't come too close, and I knew Garry's rage would surface if Tarriel got close to Odilia. But Tarriel had been raised in the pack; he knew better than to try and steal another's mate.

I spoke gently, "Odilia, that's okay. He means no harm to you."

"Are you sure?" she asked, still trembling.

Garry had a sad look when he realized he had scared her. I nodded to her.

"Werewolves can get quite possessive of their mates. Especially if another male says that they will bond with her."

Odilia looked toward Garry. All the love he held for her shone through his eyes. She looked back at me.

"What's a mate?"

Only then did Garry realize how little Odilia knew about our pack. I told her some things the other day but didn't have time to review all the details.

Seeing he was not needed anymore, Tarriel quietly took his leave. The tension in the room disappeared. Esme sat in a chair, and I sat on Odilia's bed. I explained everything to her, from the fated mates given to us by the Moon Goddess to the bond that forms between them. When I was done, Garry had already put back his t-shirt. He was softly caressing Odilia's hand. She was still gauging him. I couldn't even imagine all that was going on in her head.

Odilia looked at me, overwhelmed.

"Well, that is a lot to take in at once!"

Garry spoke softly, "I have heard about your husband's death. I'm sorry for your loss."

Odilia merely nodded to him, tremors of sadness still betraying her voice, "Garry. I don't know if I'm ready to love again. Everything is happening so fast! Just this morning, I hoped Gerald would return, and I found out he's dead."

Garry nodded. "I understand."

She continued, grief and resignation in her eyes, "I'm not sure I understand all this mate thing. But I've been told I'd die if I didn't bond with a werewolf because my baby's father was one too."

Garry kneeled in front of her.

"I would never let you die. Please, let me bond with you."

The words were so sincere that Odilia put a hand over her heart.

I told her, "You must know, the mate bond is forever. Once the bond is sealed, it cannot be undone. But also know that your mate will love you forever."

Odilia smiled faintly despite everything that had happened to her today. "My heart is broken, I'm filled with grief, and my life has been shattered. I'm not sure there's much to do with me. Many things have happened, and I need time to adjust. I'm even bearing a child that's not yours. I don't see why you'd waste your time with me."

Garry spoke passionately, "Don't say that! Whatever time you need, I will be patient. This child you are bearing, I will raise it as my own. Just let me prove that I'm a worthy mate for you. Please."

Odilia smiled at him, and he smiled back at her. They were linked in ways Odilia couldn't understand yet, and they would need to learn about each other, but in that smile, I saw hope for better days.

"I don't understand where this is coming from, but I'm willing to live and see where this new life will take me. I feel something pulling me to you, even if I don't comprehend it. How do we bond?"

Garry smirked at her question. I knew the answer, but it wasn't for me to say it.

Esme stood. "Serena and I will leave you two together. Garry can explain everything to you."

Odilia had questioning eyes, but Garry had a knowing look. I knew everything would be fine when I left the room.

DeMörder's POV

I sat on my throne. I woke up an hour ago in the forest and couldn't recall how I had gotten there. It was already dark, and I had a crushing headache. Disoriented, I wandered into the woods. It was like I could see myself walking, a strange feeling. Who could tell what was real and what was not? At one point, I stumbled on Marcus and Judah. Seeing them snapped something in my mind, getting me out of that confused state and back to normal. I walked to my chambers with them, bathed, and sat on my throne since then.

My followers were reunited before me, a few braziers emitting a yellow light. The number of worshippers has been growing steadily, and I rejoiced at the thought that I'd soon have enough to assert my vengeance. They started chanting a prayer they had created for me. Listening to their praise, I closed my eyes.

I thought back to a few weeks ago: I recalled how powerless I was. The memory was faint, somewhat blurred. I don't remember what happened before that moment, but I was sad, broken, alone, and weak. I was lost, and despair filled my soul. Hurt once more by the ones who dared to call themselves family. I had fled into this dark cave. I passed a few dark underground lakes, the air getting colder. Eventually, he was here: two black feathered wings, dark charcoal skin, and fiery-red eyes. He stood tall and strong; I could feel a dark power emanating from him. I immediately envied him. He didn't need to fear others as I did; he didn't let people hurt him. He could crush anyone. I knew then: that's who I wanted to be.

As if reading my thoughts, the demon smiled wickedly at me.

"So, you want to be like me, mortal?"

I nodded to him, the words barely escaping my mouth as my heart raced, "Yes, please."

The demon sneered.

"I can give you power… Stronger than you could ever imagine. You'll be able to crush anyone you want."

Beads of sweat formed on my forehead, and I swallowed in reverence, fear, and wonder. I knew demons didn't offer power for free.

"What do you want in exchange?"

The demon's eyes glimmered in the darkness.

"That you kill as many as possible and revive them to fight at your side."

"Revive them?" I asked in bewilderment.

The low voice of the demon echoed on the cave's walls as he answered. "I will make you a necromancer. Giving you incredible strength and the power to raise the dead. You will be able to raise an army to fulfill whatever your heart desires. Feared and respected by all."

Necromancers were strong and dreaded. History mentioned only two occurrences of necromancers. No one knows how they came to be, but a dark bond with a demon must have been their power source. Both times, they brought fear, respect, and destruction to the world. Countless died trying to stop them. Still, to this date, legends spoke of their actions. If I had this power, no one could hurt me.

But I was still wary of the demon.

"What good will it do to you if I kill people and revive them? This seems like I get the better half of the bargain."

"You're smart, mortal, but fear not. This is exactly what I need. By killing people and reviving them in your army of undead, you will keep the souls from going to the afterlife. Disrupting the soul flow is exactly what I need you to do."

His offer was interesting, the power was great, and I didn't need to give much in exchange. There were not many thoughts to put into it.

"All right, demon. How do we seal this deal?"

The demon smiled widely, showing his teeth.

"You only need to speak my name."

Just as I was about to ask what his name was, it came to my mind strong and vivid, as if I had always known.

The ground shook as I shouted his name, "Erebus."

A sharp pain resonated through my skull, and voices echoed in my mind. The sound of my screams mixed with the wicked laughter of the demon. The pain subsided for a moment as I watched myself curling on the floor, grabbing my head with both hands. My body was aching, but I didn't feel it anymore. I was but a spectator of the scene unraveling in front of me. It only lasted for a split second until I got dragged back into my body, pain searing in each of my bones.

I lay on the floor, covered in sweat, unable to move as the ache subsided. Like a newborn, I watched the world around me. Everything looked so different. I could feel the power of the demon pulse in my veins. So dark, so strong, so wicked. I turned to look at the demon, but he was gone. One thought was left in my mind. *I couldn't wait to try this newfound power.*

"Master, your disciples are waiting."

I opened my eyes at Judah's voice. My followers were all kneeling, waiting for my orders to be given. A thick fog was covering the ground tonight. A lone raven flew over my head, its caw echoing in the moment's silence. The wind picked up, bringing the scent of rotting trees to my nose before dying as quickly as it came. It may have been summer, but it felt like fall with all the dead trees. I walked back and forth on the stone plateau, my footsteps reverberating on the rocks.

"Be prepared! Tonight marks the beginning of a new era!"

I walked down the plateau between the rows of worshippers as I talked. The zombies were staring at the void in front of them. Their empty minds made me feel alone in this crowd of people. The living didn't dare look at me as I approached. A feeling of power came over me at the sight of the respect shown to me by my worshippers. I will reward them when the time comes.

I kept my head high and spoke loudly, "Now, pay attention! As this is the era of a new king! A king undisputed, respected, and seen for the wonder I am. This is the chance of a lifetime."

"I will follow you," spoke Judah with pride and conviction.

"So will I," added Marcus, a hand on his chest as he spoke.

I smiled as other followers confirmed their allegiance to me. I continued, "Of course, you're expected to take some duties on board. But you will be rewarded when I'm given my dues. After decades of injustice and denial, finally, my time has come! Be prepared!"

"I will give my life to you," whispered a woman.

"Be prepared!" chanted some men.

All around me, my disciples started chanting and worshipping me. I smiled; finally, I was given the respect that was due. Soon, everyone would know.

Matthew's POV

I was sitting by the fire with Elisen. I watched the light from the fire reflect on her purplish skin. The light from the stars made her skin shimmer a little. Her eyes shone with passion as she explained everything about soul nymphs. She had washed in a nearby river and braided her hair loosely. She looked so exotic, and I couldn't get my eyes off her. I would worship her forever, taking care of her as I should.

I still couldn't believe how weak she was when I found her. To think that if I hadn't heard her… a knot formed in my stomach at that thought. My wolf was feeling uneasy at this thought too. Now that I had found her, my wolf didn't want to let go of her, and neither did I. I held her close while she talked. Her lilac scent drove me crazy, and I had to refrain from burying my nose in the crook of her neck.

"So, when someone dies, they go to the nymph soul's realm?" asked Kelly.

"Well, it's not really a realm by itself. More like an enchanted domain where mortals can't enter. Only souls and my people can cross its borders."

"Don't people get curious?" asked Theo.

Elisen shook her head, her long hair swinging as she did.

"No. Our domain is invisible to the living. The same way you don't see the soul leaving the body when someone dies."

Learning about soul nymphs was fascinating. I wanted to learn everything about my mate. I wanted to understand her and to know about her ancestors as well.

"How do you know which souls can travel to the Elysian Plains?" I asked.

She turned toward me, her lips brushing on my cheek as she did. A soft purr escaped my chest at this contact, making her blush. She turned back to the others, explaining, "When the souls enter our domain, they stay there for a little while. Just enough for the three judges to decide on their fate."

"Three judges?" asked Kelly.

Elisen nodded. "The demigods Rhadamanthys, Minos, and Aeacus, sons of Zeus. They were once mortals but were granted their position as judges as a reward for their lives on earth."

"What happens next?" asked Kelly.

Elisen giggled at Kelly's enthusiasm. Her laugh was music to my ears, and I wanted to hear it every day.

"Well, one of the members of my clan brings the soul to the Elysian Plains or the Underworld, depending on what the judges have decided. We sometimes bring the young nymphs in training so that they learn how it must be done."

Kelly exclaimed, "Oh! The Elysian Plains must be so beautiful! You probably never want to come back from it."

Elisen shook her head vehemently. "Dear God, no! We never travel to the Elysian Plains or the Underworld ourselves. We bring the souls to the entrance and ensure they make it through the door. Only a departed soul can cross the barrier from this world to the afterlife. A few exceptions have existed throughout history, but those are anomalies."

I landed a soft kiss near her ear, whispering, "Well, I'm glad you're not traveling to the afterlife. I wouldn't want to risk losing you."

Elisen turned and stared into my eyes, smiling, before landing her smooth lips on mine, igniting a fire inside me. My wolf purred as she did.

"Where's that sound coming from?"

I smirked. "That's my wolf. He loves it when you come close like that."

Elisen's hand brushed against my chest, sparks inflaming on my skin as she did.

"He's inside of you, is he?"

I shook my head. "More or less. I am him, and he is me. My wolf is a part of me; we're one together."

"Will I ever meet him?"

My wolf wagged his tail, and I had to fight to keep in control. He wanted to meet her, but I wasn't sure if she was ready.

"When you're ready, of course, you'll meet him. I want you to know everything about me."

Kelly interrupted, "Hey, have you guys seen Gregory? I can't find him anywhere."

I looked around. I couldn't find him either. I shrugged my shoulders. "He's probably off exploring. I'm sure he'll be back soon."

Kelly was still worried. "What if he goes missing?"

Theo grabbed her hand in his. "Relax. I'm sure it's nothing. We can take a short walk around and see if we can find him if you want to."

Kelly nodded, smiling, and I watched as they walked hand in hand. I smirked. Theo would appreciate this time alone with his mate as much as I would enjoy this time alone with Elisen.

Chapter 8 (Matthew)

Unholy

It was getting harder to contain these feelings as I was now alone with Elisen. Knowing she didn't know about love, I was scared more than ever to let her know how I felt.

"Elisen, I… I need to tell you something."

She stared at me with her green eyes, and I found my heart beating even faster as she did.

"What is it?"

I had never been this scared in my whole life.

"I'm not sure how to say this. I'm not even sure how'll you'll perceive this, with you being a soul nymph. But I need to get it off my chest. The truth is, I love you, Elisen. I love you more than I ever thought possible."

Elisen's eyes widened as she whispered, "Love."

I waited nervously for her to add something else. She said that she felt something for me earlier, but I wasn't sure if she knew what love was.

She continued, "I guess it's what I feel for you. This *need* to be close to you. This attraction that's making my heart beat faster. A fleeting emotion of care, like I always want to be there for you. This warmth inside me that shimmers only for you."

I immediately relaxed at her words, relieved. I cupped her cheek in my hand.

"Yes, Elisen. That's called love."

Her emerald eyes flickered with a light for a moment. I could see my reflection and a promise of a future together in them.

"Then I love you too, Matthew."

My wolf purred at those words. She asked, "You said I was your mate, made by the Moon Goddess, especially for you."

I nodded, my nose touching hers as close as we were. My heart was hammering in my chest, and all I could think of was how much I'd yearned to close the distance between us and claim her tantalizing lips.

"Yes. A sacred bond given by the Moon Goddess. An undeniable attraction. Once the bond is sealed, it stays there forever."

I swallowed hard as I stared into her eyes, unable to hold myself back anymore. I kissed her luscious lips. She was delicious; I couldn't get enough of her. The way she whined from our touch made me want to kiss her forever.

She stared deeply into my eyes when we broke the kiss. Her words were passionate, "Teach me all about it."

A growl of need escaped my chest at those words. "Are you sure about this?"

She nodded. My wolf was fighting so hard I couldn't contain him anymore. This was all the encouragement I needed.

I whispered, "Are you ready to meet my wolf? Because he's dying to meet you."

She nodded and smiled. "I saw him earlier. He saved me from those thugs. Well, both of you did."

I smirked. "That's right. And now he wants to see you."

I took a step back and started to remove my clothes slowly. Elisen's stare was on me as I did, heat rising to her cheeks. Her stare was heavy with desire as she stared at my bare skin. It occurred to me that this might have been the first time she saw a naked man, but I couldn't back off now. My wolf was gnawing his patience for me to release him, clawing at the walls, struggling for control. When I was fully naked, I finally welcomed the change. It only lasted a few seconds, during which I could see the awe in Elisen's eyes.

My vision changed as I stared at her from my wolf's form. She was even more beautiful this way, pure energy emanating from her. Her lilac scent was mixed with her scent of arousal, and it was intoxicating me. I walked to her and rubbed my muzzle on her. The way she slid her fingers in my fur was perfect. She scratched behind my ears, making me purr in delight.

She smiled. "Hm, you like that, don't you?"

I closed my eyes, enjoying her touch. I was eager for us to get closer, so our bond formed, and I could talk to her through her mind, even in my wolf form. Right now, I couldn't communicate with her.

She added, "Your fur is so soft! I never want to stop running my fingers through it."

And I never want you to stop, I thought to myself.

She landed a kiss on top of my head, lighting a fire inside me. Now that my wolf had met her, I needed her in a way only a man could take her. I let my wolf cuddle with her again, then walked further away. My wolf was hungry for her and gladly gave me back control.

As I returned to my human form, Elisen suggested, "Maybe we should go in our tent."

I was so profoundly enticed by her that I had completely forgotten we were in the open.

I smirked. "You're right, just in case Kelly and Theo return."

I laid her gently on a mattress in our tent. I was already hard for her. As I kissed her, a question rose to my mind.

I whispered while caressing her body gently, "You said earlier that your race doesn't reproduce…."

I wasn't sure how to formulate my question. Elisen blushed, guessing what I was about to ask. Her lips nibbled gently at mine for a moment before she answered, "I can't reproduce the same way as you do. But I have reproductive organs if that's what you're asking."

I looked at her, baffled by her statement. "Yes, that's what I was wondering, but… I don't understand."

She giggled, tracing her fingers on my chest, her nails giving me goosebumps as they passed. Her words felt hot on my skin as she explained, "We share a common ancestor with other nymphs and fairies that are very fertile. The fact we work closely with the soul realm changed how we reproduce, but we still have the organs."

I moaned as she licked my neck before she kissed it. I kissed her once more, my tongue dancing with hers.

"Do they still work?"

She had a devilish smile. "I don't know, I never tried. Soul nymphs are not usually interested in love and pleasure."

"What about you?" I asked. I wanted to make sure she wanted this, although her body seemed to indicate so.

I moaned when she grabbed my cock, her eyes shining with desire. She whispered, "I don't know if it's because of the bond. I've never felt like that before, but… I need you like it's the last thing I'll ever need."

I sucked at her neck, making her moan, leaving a faint trace of my love on her skin as I did.

My voice was husky as I answered, "Then why don't we find out if those organs of yours still work?"

She nodded, then I added, "Don't worry, I'll go easy on you. Just tell me if you need me to stop at any moment."

I removed her clothes, kissing every inch of her skin. I wanted her to feel loved and desired. I wanted her first time to be everything she's ever thought it was and even more. Her beauty blew me away as I laid eyes on her body for the first time. She was perfect in every way.

Her voice was shy, "Do you like what you see?"

I looked into her eyes. Was she self-conscious?

"Elisen," I started as I returned to kiss her lips and play with her hair. "Please don't feel shy. You are the most wonderful, beautiful, perfect woman I could ever ask for. Your body is my temple, and I shall worship you like the goddess you are."

"You were staring."

I caressed her cheek gently. "Because I couldn't get over how lucky I am to have you."

She smiled at those words, and I could feel her relax.

I got back to kissing every part of her. I smirked when I realized she was already wet for me. I brushed my fingers around her flower-shaped labia, making her gasp as I did. Happy with the effect I had on her, I glided my fingers on her clit.

"Oh, yes!" she moaned in pleasure.

Watching her unravel under my touch only made me yearn for her more. As I kept pleasuring her, I gently inserted one finger in her opening, making her gasp. Like a flower's first bloom, spreading out her beauty for me to admire.

"Do you like that?"

She arched her back and breathed a breath of pleasure for an answer. I started moving my finger into her while playing with her swollen clit. She moaned hard when she climaxed, her walls pulsing around my finger.

Her voice was lustful when she spoke, "Oh, Matt! That's so good!"

I smirked. "I want you so badly right now!"

"Then take me!"

I kissed her, the tip of my cock touching her entrance as I did. "I can't. You're a virgin. I want to make sure you enjoy this moment."

"I'm sure I'll love it!"

"Patience, my love."

I inserted a second finger while playing with her clit, hearing her sweet moans. Fuck, I was so hard for her. I wanted her so badly; this was a sweet torture. She gasped when I inserted a third finger and started to thrust into her. The scent of her arousal was driving me crazy.

I couldn't hold back anymore. I figured three fingers would be enough. I kissed Elisen's sweet lips, aligning my cock with her opening, looking at her for one last confirmation. "Are you sure about this?"

She nodded. "Please, Matthew."

A growl of need escaped my chest. I wanted to pound into her but didn't want to hurt her. I inserted the tip of my cock into her, giving her time to adjust to being stretched. She gasped at the contact, digging her nails into my back. I kissed her, muffling her moans. I kept going slowly, inch by inch, gauging her reactions and ensuring she enjoyed every moment. A sweet torture of pain and love swirling in a slow waltz.

I took a pause when I was entirely inside her.

"Are you okay?"

Her breath was hot on my neck, her voice full of thirst as her words rolled on my skin in a long, passionate yearning, "Yesss."

I hissed when she thrust her hips, testing her power over me.

"Fuck, Elisen! You're so tight!"

The smirk told me how much she enjoyed this. I thrust slowly into her, her breaths quickening and her nipples brushing against me. I felt closer to her than I'd ever been. My wolf yearned to mark her as mine, but I didn't want to do it yet. We hadn't discussed this. It could wait for another day.

I licked her neck and nibbled her ear lobe, getting lost in this sea of pleasure, wave after wave washing over me. She closed her eyes, screaming in ecstasy, her walls pulsing around me as she climaxed, a delightful display of beauty and love; the feeling of it pushing me over the edge, I groaned hard as release washed over me.

I rested my forehead against hers, spent. Never have I felt connected to a woman as much as at this moment. In her smile, I could see her love. In her eyes, I could see my salvation. In her soul, I could see my future.

Surrounded by her lilac scent, my life was finally perfect. Her voice sounded in my mind, *"I can't believe how much I love you!"*

I smiled, happy to see the bond was forming between us. I pushed out my feelings for her through her mind, her eyes closing and her lips curving as she felt it.

I pushed through her mind, *"I will always protect you, provide for you, care for you. I will love you with all that I am, forever."*

She looked at me in awe, whispering, "I can hear you."

I nodded. "Yes, because you're my mate. Our bond will only get stronger."

"This feeling, it's wonderful. There are no words for it."

I kissed her sweet lips again. "I know; I feel it too."

I lay by Elisen's side, passing my arms around her, holding her close. She cuddled with me, and I buried my nose in the crook of her neck, whispering, "Sleep well, my love."

I woke up in the morning, startled by some screams.

It was Gregory's voice, "Guys! Get up quickly!"

My mind raced, were we attacked? Something must have been going on for him to scream like that. Elisen and I got up as quickly as we could and got dressed. Kelly and Theo were already outside with Gregory when exited our tent.

"Gregory! We looked everywhere for you!" Kelly screamed.

Gregory's clothes were all filthy. He had dirt all over his face. He looked disheveled, and I'd doubt his mental health if I didn't know him. His eyes had a glary stare to them as he spoke.

"Oh my god! You guys don't know what I saw last night!"

Elisen grabbed my hand as we all hung on Gregory's lips, eagerly waiting to hear his story.

"I was walking further southwest, scouring the area, when I heard a noise. I crouched and saw the dead walking! I swear to you! Disassembled corpses dragging their limbs about just as you and I walk!"

"What?" interrupted Kelly in disbelief.

"That's impossible!" added Theo.

"That's unholy…," whispered Elisen.

"I swear to you! I saw them with my own eyes!" cried Gregory, passion filling his voice. "But that's not all…."

"What more could there be?" asked Kelly.

Gregory swallowed, and we all bent closer to him as he whispered, "I followed them. Hidden in the bushes… That's when I saw him! A necromancer! He's the one responsible for the missing people!"

Kelly gasped at his words. Elisen squeezed my arm in fright.

"Nonsense!" screamed Theo.

"There have been only a few occurrences of necromancers throughout the ages," I spoke calmly. "Are you sure of what you're saying?"

Gregory nodded. "Yes! I'll show you! So that you can see for yourselves."

I nodded to him. That would be the best way for everyone to believe him. It implied such power and darkness that it was better to see for ourselves.

We quickly ate breakfast and packed our things. We followed Gregory, who seemed to remember where he had been last night. After walking for a while, I noticed that the bark of the trees was black. No more leaves or birds were singing, only dark trees, dirt, and bare roots sticking out of the ground. There was an eerie silence between us as we were all absorbed in our thoughts.

As we arrived at a cliff, Gregory gestured for us to hide in the bush. My heart was racing as we waited in silence. Suddenly, a low grunt filled the air, and soon enough, dead people were walking a little further from the bushes we were hiding in. My heart raced, and I felt Elisen's worry through our bond. I couldn't believe it, but I was seeing it with my own eyes. The dead were walking.

"I told you," whispered Gregory.

"Fuck!" cursed Kelly.

"What should we do?" asked Theo before adding, "Maybe we could take them on."

Gregory shook his head.

"I saw them last night. There are hundreds of them. We can't kill them all by ourselves."

"We go back to the pack. We need to report this to the Alpha," I ordered. They all nodded to me.

We started getting back in silence, trying not to disturb the zombies. Just as we thought we were getting to a reasonable distance from them, a tall, blonde zombie stood in front of us. The blood ran cold through my veins when I saw the scar on the woman's face. I knew from the "L" shape of the scar that it was Molly's mother. Thoughts raced in my mind. *What would happen to Molly? We couldn't tell her that her mother was a zombie. We'd need to think of something.*

But first, we needed to deal with Theresa. She was pissed at us and didn't intend to let us go back to the pack. Luckily, we were far enough from the other zombies to go undetected. If they all saw us, we'd be in trouble. She started swinging her fists at Theo.

"They're supposed to be slow, right?" asked Kelly. "Let's outrun her!"

It was a good idea. How fast could a reanimated corpse run? We started to sprint toward our pack, but Theresa was just behind us.

Elisen shrieked when the zombie grabbed her hand. A menacing growl escaped my chest, and I let my wolf take control. There was no way I was allowing a zombie to attack my mate.

I jumped on Theresa and bit her arm with force. It didn't bother her; she held Elisen's hand firmly.

Kelly and Theo joined us and attacked Theresa, but she only grunted in response and tried to scratch and bite them. Elisen grabbed one of her swords with her free hand and stabbed the zombie in the shoulder, but despite the sword being made of a soul-severing metal, it didn't seem to bother Theresa. I wondered if she still had a soul, but there was no time to ponder it.

"How do you even kill what's already dead?" asked Theo.

Rage filled me; I wanted my mate free from the zombie. My animal instincts took hold of me. That thing had to die. I locked my teeth in the zombie's arm and shook violently with all my strength. The arm ripped from Theresa's body, the hand finally letting go of Elisen. I dropped the arm to the floor, but the zombie didn't mind. It was already dead; missing an arm was only bothersome for her.

I pushed through Elisen's mind, *"Are you okay?"* She was my main concern, and my wolf wouldn't let me concentrate on the battle unless I was sure she was okay.

"I am, thanks, Matt," she pushed back.

Only then did I turn back toward the living corpse before us.

"Won't the necromancer revive her if we kill her?" asked Gregory.

Theo cursed, "I think you're right!"

"No!" shouted Elisen. "The necromancer must be in the right range to revive her."

"Okay, but how do we kill it? She seems fine even without an arm," pointed out Kelly.

Theo snorted, "I'd like to see her try to fight without a head."

I snickered at his remark to myself; this was the best plan we had. Kelly changed into her wolf while Theo grabbed his long-sword. Elisen had her two swords, and Gregory fought with his fists as best he could. Kelly and I charged at the zombie with our claws, tearing up the undead's flesh. She was powerful despite being undead and missing an arm. Theo finally swung his sword with both arms, giving him momentum, and managed to cut the zombie's head off.

We all stopped moving, watching the body falling to the floor now that its head was severed. Gregory was shaking, in shock. I was wary, half expecting the body to return to life again. A feeling of grief overcame me when a few seconds passed, and it was still dead. This was Molly's mother. She was now officially an orphan, having lost both of her parents. I didn't know how I'd tell her the news. Should I even tell her? I had failed my promise to her. I was supposed to bring back her mother, not kill her. Although she was already dead when I found her, did it make it right to kill her a second time?

"Who's Molly?" asked Elisen through our bond.

The words came to me without thinking, *"My adoptive daughter."*

I didn't know why I said that. It wasn't entirely true, and Molly didn't know it yet. But when I met her, I knew I wanted to be there for this child. And now that both of her parents were gone, I knew deep in my soul that I would be her new father.

"You're full of surprises!" exclaimed Elisen in my mind.

I looked at her as I transformed back into my human form. Elisen was smiling.

"I even surprise myself sometimes," I answered back.

She put her hands behind my neck, kissing my lips.

"It will take time for me to adjust to this."

I grabbed her hips, bringing her closer.

"Do you still want me? Knowing I have this child to care for?"

She giggled. "Of course! Why would it change anything to what I feel for you?"

I didn't know what to answer. Of course, I didn't expect it to change anything about her feelings, and Elisen was also my fated mate. But caring for a kid was a lot of responsibilities. And it was all happening so fast! Even for me!

Elisen brushed her lips on my neck, getting me out of my thoughts.

"I'll just need a little time to get used to this."

I nodded. The only words I could find were those of my heart, "I love you, Elisen."

When everyone was ready, we started walking back toward the pack. We needed to warn everyone about the necromancer and the zombies.

Chapter 9 (Serena)

Ceremonial Scepter

Odilia's condition had been improving rapidly after Garry had bonded with her. She had moved into his home and was able to live normally. Garry was outside the house chopping wood when I arrived, his long blond hair soaked, sweat dripping down his forehead from the effort. His t-shirt was stuck to his chest from sweat, showing his muscles. I had to admit Odilia's mate was handsome. Would I ever find mine?

He put his axe down when he saw me. "Hi, Serena!"

I waved to him. "Hi! Is Odilia home?"

He swiped the sweat from his forehead with the bottom of his t-shirt, showing his abs.

"Yes. Go on, make yourself at home. She'll be happy to see you."

I tried not to drool at the sight of his abs and smiled. "Thanks!"

Garry and Odilia lived in a small wooden house. The front door opened into an open space containing the living and dining rooms. Sofas and a small library filled with books filled the living room. A table filled the dining room, and the dark wooden cabinets in the kitchen could be seen from where I stood. All of this contrasted with the yellow curtains on the windows, giving the room a nice, colorful touch.

Odilia was sitting at the table when I entered the house. A bouquet of roses was sitting on the table, letting its pleasant scent waft through the house. Right next to the roses was a teddy bear. A gift for her future child.

Odilia didn't hear me when I entered the house. She was too focused on the little book she was writing in.

"I didn't know you were an author," I said as I entered the house.

She looked up and smiled when she saw it was me.

"That? Oh, that's only my poetry journal."

"A poetry journal?" I asked as I took a seat by her side.

"Yes. I keep it with me all the time. It's the only thing I brought when I left my house. It helps me deal with all those emotions."

"It sounds like a good way to cope with everything happening."

She nodded. "One day, I dream of publishing it."

I spoke with wonder in my voice, "Odilia's Poetry Journal. That sounds grand!"

She giggled. "Thanks. Maybe I'll have the courage to do it one day. To open up my feelings to everyone. It's my own way of telling my journey."

"If you ever do, please tell me. I'd love to grab a copy."

She grinned. "Deal!"

"I came to see how you were doing," I added.

She got up and put the kettle on the fire to prepare tea.

"As you can see, I'm doing better. I can walk around and do what I want again. My body has adjusted to the baby."

Curiosity got the better of me. "How was it? To bond with Garry?" As I spoke the words, I wondered if she was comfortable talking about it. I added quickly, "If it's not too personal."

She laughed. "That's okay. I don't mind."

She took a moment to think before answering.

"I was initially scared when Garry told me he needed to bite me. He said couples usually did so in an intimate moment, but he understood we barely knew each other, which was a relief! I wasn't ready for that!"

Water boiled, and Odilia stopped to prepare our tea. Her belly was starting to show, and she radiated a glow that all expecting mothers seemed to share.

She sat by my side to continue her tale. "Garry was gentle and delicate. He surrounded me in kisses and tenderness, soothing my sadness. He even warned me before biting. The pain didn't last long, and an overwhelming feeling filled me before I could even think about it. An unconditional love, pleasure, and the feeling that I always belonged with him. Just like that, as if I had always known him."

"That must have been nice," I commented.

She nodded. "At first, I felt confused. I had just learned about the death of my husband and about the fact that he was a werewolf. I barely knew Garry. I didn't understand how I could feel like that or be so peaceful. But Garry explained that it was because I was his fated mate. He then closed his eyes, and my mind was flooded with images: the Moon Goddess, the origins of your pack, werewolves, magic, fated mates, and the demon. Instantly, I truly understood the strength of that bond and accepted that my future was with Garry."

I smiled at her words. "I'm glad to know you're feeling at peace."

Odilia took a sip of her tea. "It doesn't mean I don't think of Gerald occasionally. I still wish my child's father was there, which still pains me. But I know Garry will be there for the child and me. I know he will be a wonderful father. I learn more about him daily and fall in love with him every passing hour."

Just as she spoke, Garry entered the house. He looked at Odilia like she was the world's most precious jewel. He kissed and hugged her as he got to the table, then said, "Serena. Esme is looking for you. She sent fairies to look for you."

"Oh!" I exclaimed, "I'll go to her house right away!"

Garry shook his head. "She's at the pack's house. I'm going as well. It seems Matthew and Kelly are back, and they discovered something."

"Really?" asked Odilia. "Then I want to go too. I'm part of the pack now."

Garry nodded. "Let's all go together, then."

I downed the rest of my tea, and we all left for the pack's house.

Alpha David and Esme were talking with Kelly, Matthew, Theo, Gregory, and a woman I had never seen when we arrived at the pack's house. They looked agitated. Molly was holding Matthew's hand while he talked with the Alpha.

"I'm telling you! I saw them with my own eyes. The dead are walking," exclaimed Matthew to his father.

A knot formed in my stomach at these words, and Odilia found refuge in Garry's arms.

"We even had an encounter with one of them!" added Kelly, agitated.

David and Esme looked overwhelmed.

Gregory added, "There's a necromancer. He's the one responsible. I saw him!"

Molly grabbed her head with both hands, screaming, "Stop it!"

Everyone stared at the little girl. Tears were flowing down her cheeks.

Matthew kneeled at her level. "What is it, honey?"

The child sniffled. "The man in the wall. He keeps saying he'll kill you all. He says you're messing with his servant and their plan."

We were all shocked. Matthew took the little girl in his arms, lovingly protecting her.

He asked her, "Is the man in the wall responsible for the undead?"

The little girl shook her head.

"No, the man in the wall is his master."

I covered my mouth at that sentence, and tears welled up in my eyes. It confirmed what Tarriel had said about the undead. But I kept wondering who the man in the wall was. A necromancer was powerful enough. Who could be his master?

Matthew whispered to Molly, but the room's silence allowed us to hear, "No one will kill us. We will stay with you."

Kelly was about to add something when Alpha David gestured.

"It's okay. I believe you."

Silence filled the room for a while. We waited for the Alpha's order, but he wasn't talking. Esme spoke with wisdom, "I think we should all gather in the war-thinking room and plan our next actions."

The Alpha nodded to her, and everyone walked toward the war-thinking room.

As I started following them, Molly pulled on Matthew's hand, walking toward me. Her eyes were now dry, but you could see she had cried.

"Serena!"

I smiled at her.

"Hi there, Molly!"

She released Matthew's hand to hug me. I hugged her before greeting Matthew.

"Hi, Matthew. It's nice to see you."

"Likewise," he answered before adding, "Meet Elisen, my mate."

I smiled at those words. It meant this woman was to be my future Luna when Matthew would replace his father as the Alpha. I bowed slightly. "It's an honor to meet you."

Elisen seemed uncomfortable with my reaction. "Please, I'm no queen. I'm just a simple soul nymph."

I had never heard of soul nymphs, but now I was curious more than ever to learn about them. I hoped I'd get the opportunity to ask Elisen about her people.

Matthew shook his head. "Nonsense. As my mate, you are the next Luna of the pack. It's normal for people to show their respect. I expect nothing less from them." Then he gestured to me. "Serena is one of the best spell casters of the pack."

Honor filled me at those words. To get the recognition of my future Alpha was a big deal!

Elisen nodded. "Nice to meet you, Serena."

Molly pulled on Matthew's hand. "The man in the wall says you found my mom."

Elisen and Matthew's faces changed at those words. Molly asked, "Did you find my mom?"

Matthew kneeled on the floor, looking into the little girl's eyes. "I'm sorry, Molly. We saw your mom, but...." He took a moment, trying to find his words. "She won't be coming back to you. I'm sorry."

The little girl sniffed, speaking in a high-pitched voice, "Is she dead?"

Matthew whispered, "Yes, Molly. She is."

The little girl started crying, finding comfort in Matthew's arms. Seeing him like that, I couldn't help but think he would make a great father and would be a great Alpha.

Molly started singing softly, "… for rain has a little silver dew and trees arbor all fruits. All your fears will vanish. Forget your worries, and follow me."

Elisen was taken aback, and she kneeled by their side.

"Molly, where have you heard this song?" she asked in surprise.

The little girl answered, "It's a song mommy used to sing to me."

"That… can't be!" Elisen exclaimed.

"What's the matter?" I asked.

"That's the song we sing to guide the souls to the Elysian Plains. It is passed down from one generation of soul nymphs to another."

I answered, "Then Molly's mother must have been a soul nymph, just like you."

Elisen shook her head. "That's impossible! Soul nymphs don't reproduce."

Matthew smiled, his words filled with tenderness, "Well, maybe you can, but you didn't know."

Elisen pointed to one of the walls of the halls.

"Molly, tell me. What do you see?"

The little girl looked where Elisen was pointing. I looked, but I couldn't see anything but a regular wall.

But Molly answered, "A light, glowing white, flowing like water. It starts near the ceiling and goes into the wall further."

I would have considered it to be the girl's imagination if it hadn't been for Elisen's shocked face.

She whispered, "She can see the flow of souls… There can be no mistake. One of her parents had to be a soul nymph."

Matthew smiled and grabbed Molly in his arms, hugging her. She buried her nose in his neck, whispering, "I love you."

Matthew kissed the little girl's cheek, then said to Elisen, "You know what that means, right?"

Still stunned, she looked at him. "I never dared to think it was even possible."

He brought her closer with Molly still in his arms. "Well, I'm glad it is."

Elisen answered, "But I don't know about any man in the wall."

Molly frowned. "Stop laughing, you meanie!"

Elisen looked at her. "Are you talking to the man in the wall?"

The child nodded.

"Can you tell me who he is? Can you describe him to me?"

Molly answered, "He's very dark and mean. His eyes glow red, but I can't see him very well. He follows me. He says I'm special."

Elisen stared at me, then at Matthew with wide eyes. Matthew told the child, "Don't worry. We won't let him get to you."

David entered the room. "I thought you guys would already be in the war-thinking room. We're waiting for you to start."

Matthew apologized, "Sorry, Dad. It's my fault. We're coming."

We all nodded and followed the Alpha to the war-thinking room.

The tiles in the war-thinking room were worn out and dusty. The drapes were tied to the side to let the sun's lukewarm light enter the room. This room had no decorations; it was made for strategy and decision-making. It was my second time coming here, as it was usually reserved for the Alpha and the generals. But as a talented spell caster, I had been invited here the last time a war occurred with some werewolf pack wanting to take over our territory. The map of the region was hung on the wall, and a few crucial places were marked on it. On the big, wooden table laid a few flags, daggers, and everything needed to write. A pitcher full of water was at the center of the table. The Alpha already had a goblet in his hand.

David pointed to the map. "Where did you see this necromancer?" he asked Gregory.

Gregory stood and pointed to the southwest. "There. That's where I saw him."

David pinned a small flag at the location on the map. It was further than the pack's territory.

He breathed. "The pack will be moving soon, but we're not ready yet. We must deal with this threat, or it will hinder us."

Matthew rose. "I will go, Father. As the future Alpha, it is my duty to protect the pack."

David nodded. "I wouldn't expect less of you, Son."

I stood along with Kelly, Theo, Elisen, and Gregory.

I spoke, "It would be an honor to join you."

Esme shook her head. "I'm sorry, Serena. I need you to do something more important."

"What could be more important than to deal with this threat?" I asked.

"You need to secure the ceremonial scepter."

I froze at those words and didn't argue. I knew she was right. The ceremonial scepter was powerful, and we needed to ensure it didn't fall into the wrong hands.

Esme added, "But fear not, I shall dispatch four of our spell casters to assist Matthew in his task."

I sat down, disappointed that I couldn't help Matthew but happy to know spell casters would be part of the journey.

Gregory eagerly shouted. "I want to go too!"

David spoke with authority, "I'm sorry, Gregory. You can't go with them. This will be very dangerous. I will dispatch some of our best werewolves' fighters for this."

Gregory stuttered, "But… but… I can still help!"

But the Alpha refused his request, "This is for your own good, son."

Gregory sat back, defeated.

Esme gestured for me to follow her. Seeing Gregory feeling sad, I put a hand on his shoulder.

"Come on, don't be sad. I'm not going either."

He looked at me. "But at least you have a task to do. You're useful."

I bit my lower lip. I understood how Gregory felt.

"Why don't you come with Esme and me? Maybe you can help with the scepter?"

Gregory's mood lightened up. "You really think so?"

The truth was that magic needed to be involved in securing the scepter. But if I could make him feel helpful, I'd be happy to have him there.

I smiled and nodded. "Yes! I'm sure you will help us greatly!"

Esme was surprised when she saw Gregory with me but didn't say anything. We followed her to a room at the back of the pack's house. There, she opened a locked chest.

I gasped at the sight of the ceremonial scepter. The handle was made of carved gold. The pommel was elongated and made of glass, encased in intricate gold leaves. Inside was a blue magic crystal. The top of the pommel was also surrounded by gold leaves. It was shaped like a diamond, letting the blue glow of the crystal shine through every facet of the glass. I could feel its power without even touching it.

A sense of panic washed over me when Gregory lunged forward to grab it. He was too fast, and I couldn't stop him. A second later, he was thrown back by the scepter's energy.

"What the?" he asked as he landed on the floor.

Esme scolded him, "You can't touch the ceremonial scepter. Its magic is mighty."

"How can anyone steal it, then?" asked Gregory.

Esme helped him up.

"People who know about the scepter have the power necessary to steal it." Then she turned to me. "Serena, conceal it."

I took a profound inspiration. I needed a lot of concentration to conceal such a powerful object. The scepter didn't want to be hidden; it wanted to be found. I'd need to fight against its magic to succeed.

I closed my eyes and concentrated on the spell, *"Occultare, abscondo, celo, concelo...."* As magic filled me, I could feel the scepter's magic fight against me, like a strong wind trying to push me. I kept my hands straight, pushing back the wind. I gradually molded an eggshell of concealing magic, building it piece by piece. As the shell formed around the scepter, its magic concentrated, making it harder to fight against. Just like when fluids flow into a narrower space, it speeds up; the same happened with the scepter's magic. I had to push with my two hands, my hair blowing in the air, as I closed the remaining hole, making the shell around the scepter complete.

I opened my eyes. I was out of breath. Gregory had questioning eyes, but Esme knew.

"What just happened?" he asked. "I don't see anything different."

I smirked. "That's because you can't see it with your eyes."

Esme gestured to me. I walked forth and grabbed the scepter; its magic couldn't do anything to me since there was an outer shell around it. Gregory looked at me in awe.

"Wow! That's amazing, Serena!"

I grinned. "Thanks."

Esme instructed us, "Now, you should go to the chapel."

"The chapel?" I repeated. "Why?"

"Because that's where you'll lock the scepter."

"Why aren't we keeping it in the pack's house anymore?" asked Gregory.

Esme answered, "Many people are in the pack's house while we prepare to move. It will be safer to keep it in the chapel. Fewer people go there."

"But won't it be exposed?" I retorted.

Esme shook her head. "We will station guards at the chapel and keep the scepter's location secret. Everyone will still think it's at the pack's house. That should keep prying eyes away. Besides…" She paused and gave me a look. "You know where to put it."

I nodded. I knew exactly what she was talking about. Gregory was listening attentively.

Esme added, "Of course, Serena will cast a locking spell on the scepter."

I nodded to her. It was a good plan. I didn't dare to ask what we'd do when the pack moved away, but that question could wait.

I walked to the chapel with Gregory. I carried the scepter hidden in a blanket to avoid attracting attention. The sun was already low on the horizon. The chapel wasn't that grand in itself. From the outside, it looked like a slightly bigger house than the others. The main difference was the tower to its right.

Gregory asked, "So, how will we hide the scepter?"

I shushed him, "Don't talk about it. We need to keep it secret!"

I looked around us, and hopefully, there was no one.

"Right," whispered Gregory. "What do you need me to do?"

I knew he only wanted to help, but there was nothing for him to do, really. I was only letting him tag along so he could feel useful. I noticed there weren't any guards in front of the chapel yet.

"You must guard the chapel's entrance while I hide this."

"What?" he asked. "How's that even helping? I thought we were a team!"

"But we are a team!" I exclaimed. "It's vital no one knows about this. So your job is very important."

Gregory thought for a moment. "Oh, I see! Okay, it sounds like a good plan."

Relieved, I walked into the chapel alone while Gregory stood at the entrance.

The chapel's interior was beautiful, and I was always amazed whenever I came in. What you thought was two floors from the outside was actually one floor with a double-height ceiling. Sculpted columns adorned the walls, and the floor was engraved with prayers to the Moon Goddess. At the far end of the room stood a magical altar. It stood on a round, silver pedestal. The altar had been sculpted in silver and gold, molded by magic. Three feet shaped like leaves held it in place. It started with silver at the base and then changed to gold. The top of it was shaped like a bird of paradise flower. The petals were made of gold. At the center of it was one taller petal made with blue crystal, the light from the sun passing through it, making it glow. Overall it was beautiful, and the flower's heart was the perfect place to hide the scepter. It could be magically sealed, and no one would even notice it.

I walked to the pedestal and pronounced the sacred words taught by the Moon Goddess, passed down from witch to witch throughout the ages. The petals of the pedestal moved, revealing a hollow gap at the center.

I pulled the scepter from the blanket and placed it at the center. I concentrated and removed the shell I had cast earlier. It might have sounded counterintuitive, but the fact was, we wanted the scepter's magic to be activated. This way, if anyone were to try to take the scepter without having the proper powers, he would get thrown off, just like Gregory had been. When it was done, I finally cast a locking spell on the scepter, making it even harder for someone to steal it.

I began to chant the sacred words again. The petals began to return to their original position, hiding the relic they now contained. Three teenagers burst into the room as I spoke the words, followed by Gregory.

"Stop! You can't enter!" Gregory shouted.

"Like you can do anything to stop us!" Teased one of the teenagers.

"Useless Gregory!" shouted another one.

The third one laughed wickedly.

For a moment, I wondered if they had seen me or heard the sacred words. What should I do if they had seen me? This had to stay in the utmost secrecy. How could we ensure this was kept secret? Would Esme need me to kill them? I certainly hoped it wouldn't be so!

"What are you doing here?" I shouted, imbuing magic into my voice to make it sound more impressive.

The three teenagers stopped dead in their tracks. Gregory caught up to them.

"I'm sorry, Serena. I tried to stop them, but I couldn't."

I looked at them sternly, and they took a step back. I wasn't as strong as the Alpha or Esme, but my reputation as a spell caster preceded me. The younger members of the pack generally respected me.

"You three need to leave now! And if you should speak of what you've seen here tonight, I will need to report you to the Alpha and the grand witch. I don't think you'd like that, would you?"

The first one stuttered, "N-No. It w-won't be necessary."

The second one added, "So-sorry for interrupting."

The third one didn't say anything. They all ran back out of the chapel. I only hoped this scared them enough that they would keep their mouths shut.

I walked to Gregory, who was still looking at the pedestal.

"I'm sorry I couldn't keep them away," he spoke sadly.

"That's okay, Gregory. Don't worry about it. You worked hard. Go home and rest. I'll report to Esme and rest, too."

He looked at me worriedly. "You won't mention this to Esme, will you?"

I smiled at him. "As long as those three keep their mouths shut, this will be our little secret."

Gregory smiled, relieved. I knew he was only doing his best. I wouldn't expose his failure to Esme if I didn't have to.

I was glad that two guards had taken their posts at the entrance when we walked out of the chapel.

Chapter 10 (Matthew)

Stolen

My father spoke with a strong voice, "Then it's settled. You'll leave in the morning to fight this necromancer. A team of fighters will be waiting for you."

I stood, but a small hand pulled on mine.

"Are you going away?" asked Molly in a small voice.

I nodded. "I am."

She grabbed my leg, squeezing it as firmly as she could.

"Don't go! I don't want to lose you too. I'm scared."

I kneeled down and grabbed the child in my arms. My father joined us.

"I promise you will not lose me, sweetie."

My father had an amused look on his face. Elisen stood by my side.

"Dad, I want you to meet Elisen, my mate."

He smiled proudly, "It's a pleasure to meet my daughter-in-law."

Elisen blushed, not knowing what to answer. I guess they didn't have this hierarchical order within her clan.

She answered through my mind, *"We only have the Queen ordering around."*

I pushed back through her mind, *"Don't worry. My father is a nice man."*

She relaxed at my words and answered shyly, "The pleasure is mine."

My father nodded, and I added, "And this is Molly. Her parents are dead, but I will not leave her alone."

The little girl asked shyly, "Will you be my daddy?"

I nodded. "Yes, Molly. I will be your daddy. And Elisen will be your mommy."

The child hugged me, a wet kiss landing on my cheek. My heart warmed at the feeling of pure love coming from the child.

My father commented, "Seeing I have a grandchild is nice."

The little girl only turned her head to look at my father. She stayed cuddled in my arms as if afraid I'd disappear if she were to let go.

I whispered to Molly, "Tomorrow, I need to leave. But my father will look after you. I will be back, I promise."

The child only nodded.

My father smiled. "Well, it seems your life changed rapidly."

I chuckled. "Yes, but I couldn't be happier."

I spoke to Molly, "Come on, little miss. Let's find you a fitting room. When the pack moves to a new place, I promise we'll get our own house."

She kissed my cheek, whispering, "I love you, Daddy."

I hugged her tightly as my wolf purred with love. I had met Elisen and Molly by chance. Yet, I couldn't imagine living without them now. My life was complete, and I'll do everything I can to protect them. I couldn't wait to be done with the necromancer and to start a future with them.

Elisen and I put Molly in an empty guest room. Her room was next to mine, so she wouldn't be far away. My wolf was growing wary of the "man in the wall" she kept talking about. I didn't like the fact he thought she was special.

Seeing Elisen care for Molly only made me eager to have my own child. Knowing Molly's mother was probably a soul nymph gave me hope that it could become true. But Molly would always keep her place in my heart, even if I wasn't her biological father. There was no such thing as chance; fate had brought her to me.

Elisen let out a tired sigh as she dropped onto the bed next to me.

"A lot has happened today!"

I rolled to my side, cupping her cheek with my hand. "True, but I can accomplish anything with you by my side."

"I never imagined I'd be a mother," she breathed.

"Are you happy that you are? Do you resent me for dragging you into this?"

"Oh my gosh, no! I'm not mad at you. I'm thrilled that I met you and Molly. I just never dreamed it was possible!"

At those words, a purr of satisfaction escaped my chest, and Elisen smiled.

"Then I am the luckiest wolf in the world."

Her sweet lips parted when I kissed her. She quivered under my touch, her fingers clawing at my back, lighting a fire inside me. Her breath was hot on my neck, and my eyes flickered. My wolf wanted to make her ours.

My voice was heavy with desire as I spoke, "Elisen. I can barely hold him in anymore."

She put her hand on my chest, feeling my muscles. A thought flashed in my mind of her hand gliding down further, a shiver of desire taking hold of me. Surely, she could already feel my arousal.

"Your wolf?" she asked while laying kisses on my skin, driving me crazy.

I nodded, fighting to keep whatever control I had left of my body. "Yes. He wants me to make you ours. I want to seal the bond with you, Elisen. So that we spend eternity together."

She bit her lower lip as desire glowed in her eyes.

"Hm…" she started, thrusting her hip seductively at me. I grunted from the contact. All I wanted to do was to rip her clothes off.

"And what would you need to do to seal the bond?"

I licked her neck as I whispered in her ear. I thrust my cock at her opening through our clothes. A soft moan escaped Elisen's lips as I did.

"First, I'll give you shivers and pleasure until you scream my name. Then, I'll bite you where the neck meets the shoulder. That's the place where the mark will be. A mark that forever tells you're mine, sealing the bond between us."

The mewling sound from her mouth drove whatever control I had left away. I kissed my way down her body and removed her panties. The scent of her arousal was enticing. She was already wet for me, but I needed an answer from her.

I kissed her pussy, whispering, "I need to know if you're okay with this, Elisen. My wolf is driving me crazy."

She arched her back, pushing her pussy to my mouth, pleading, "Hm… Please."

I kept kissing her pussy, never touching the parts where she needed it. "Not before you answer me, love. I need you to say it. Say you'll be mine. Will you let me mark you?"

Her breathing accelerated as I kept teasing her in the most delicious way, never quite giving her what she wanted.

She moaned, "Yes! Matthew, take me. Make me yours. I want this!"

I smirked and licked my lips at her answer. She was such a good girl, and I intended to give her the release she sought. My wolf wanted me to take her already, but I wanted to take my sweet time.

I sucked and licked at her clit, making her moan. Seeing her writhe from pleasure was making me desire her even more. Her breathing was quickening, and I could feel how close she was to ecstasy. I inserted a finger in her opening while sucking and licking her clit. My cock was rock hard, and I couldn't wait to remove my pants. She gasped and moaned as I continued my endeavors until she finally came, her legs shaking, her lips calling my name.

I couldn't wait more. I needed her now. I removed my shirt. Just as I was about to remove my pants, a loud banging came at the door.

"Matthew!"

Elisen dragged the sheets up, gasping at the sudden noise. I wanted to ignore it, my cock still hard with desire. The banging continued, and the voice called again, "Open up, Matthew!"

That's when I realized it was my father. I knew I couldn't ignore this. A growl of anger escaped my chest, but I had to get the door.

Pushing back my wolf and trying to hide my erection, I opened the door slightly.

"Quick, Matthew! The ceremonial scepter has been stolen."

This news was enough to bring me back to reality.

I shouted, "What? How could it be?"

"They attacked the chapel. The necromancer and the undead. Somehow they succeeded in getting the relic."

"I thought no one knew?"

My father swung his arm in the air.

"It doesn't matter how it happened. You must recover it quickly before the necromancer learns how to use it."

I nodded. "Right. Give me a minute, and we'll be downstairs."

I closed the door and turned to Elisen. "Sorry, my love. It will have to wait."

She had a knowing look. "That's okay, I understand."

She quickly got dressed, and we got downstairs. My father was there with one of our lookouts.

"They went into the forest, to the southwest, my Alpha."

"Figures. All right, Matthew. I couldn't get people ready on such short notice, but they're waking up as we speak. They'll be instructed to join you guys on the way."

I nodded to him. "Right. We'll go now. Just take care of Molly if we're not back by dawn."

My father smiled. "Of course, I'll care for your daughter, my son."

I ran out with Elisen. I clearly remembered the place we had encountered the zombies earlier. It was the new moon, and the forest was dark. Only a few stars shone as if the night itself knew how dire the situation was. As we advanced in the woods, we soon met some zombies. Luckily, the ones we encountered were weak. Now that we knew that severing their heads was an effective way to dispose of them, we could eliminate them quickly.

We tried to avoid them as much as possible, as the real goal was to find the scepter. Finally, I spotted one powerful-looking zombie in possession of the relic. He was surrounded by four other zombies. One of them had his skull open, and his brain was showing. He limped, with a stake piercing his back, hindering his walk. I wondered for a moment how a mere zombie could hold the relic.

I was expecting to find the necromancer. I had always heard that the scepter was protected by strong energy. Only powerful casters were able to hold it. But it didn't matter now, and I pushed those thoughts away.

Elisen's voice resonated through my mind, *"We need to get ahead of them, to block their path."*

Heat radiated through my chest, and I smiled. I was happy that our bond was forming, allowing us to speak to one another.

"Let's do this!" I pushed through her mind. I transformed into my wolf form, not even taking time to remove my clothes beforehand. Changing while running was a difficult feat, but I had mastered it after years of practice. Many werewolves didn't bother to learn it, but I felt it was important to do it, and tonight it proved useful.

I couldn't shake the feeling of being observed, but I didn't have the time to check. In one big leap, I jumped in front of the group. The zombies stopped, startled. Just as they were about to turn and go back in the other direction, Elisen got behind them. Ambushed, the zombies took a fighting stance. Five against two sounded risky.

I pushed through Elisen's mind, *"Concentrate on the one that has the scepter. If he can hold it, then you should be able to too. Once you have it, we run for it."*

She didn't answer, but I could feel she understood.

I started biting and attacking the four zombies surrounding the one with the scepter. I wanted to catch their attention so that Elisen could snatch the scepter from the other. I bit and scratched at the zombies. They were powerful but slow and clumsy. When one of them turned to go after Elisen, I'd jump on it to divert its attention.

Elisen was slashing at the zombie holding the scepter, but it didn't affect him. I bit the zombie with a stake in his back on the neck, getting him on the ground. Shaking hard, I heard his neck crack. The zombie stayed on the floor, seemingly dead. Satisfied, I jumped on another zombie, slashing and biting at him, when the dead zombie suddenly rose again. That could only mean that the necromancer was nearby reviving his zombies. When I tried to scan the woods to find the necromancer, Elisen screamed, "I have it! Run!"

I turned around and saw that she had slashed the arms of the zombie that was holding the scepter and stolen the relic before he could grab it again. I bit the zombies, trying to slow them down, giving Elisen more of a head start, before running myself. When we were far away and couldn't see them anymore, we took a breath, and I changed back to my human form.

I asked Elisen, "How's the scepter? Can you hold it well?"

She nodded. "Yes, but it's surrounded by some kind of dark energy. I'd like to get rid of it as soon as possible."

I studied it. A thin, black shroud surrounded the ceremonial scepter. I supposed this was what was blocking the relic's magic, allowing us to hold it in our hands.

An out-of-breath voice startled us, "Hey! There you are, guys!"

Gregory was standing in front of us, all dirty.

"Gregory! What are you doing here?" I asked.

"I came to help!" he answered. "I was looking for you guys. I wanted to get the scepter back from those who had stolen it."

I was surprised that Gregory had caught up with us. Then I remembered that my father was supposed to send reinforcements to help us, but I couldn't see them anywhere.

"Are the others coming?" I asked.

Gregory seemed lost. "I'm not sure. Whom are you talking about?"

His answer seemed strange. I thought my father had sent Gregory to lead the troops this way. But now I wondered if he had decided to come here alone.

"Never mind," I said to Gregory. "We have the scepter. Let's get back to the pack's house."

"Great!" he exclaimed. "Can I bring it back?"

I looked at him warily. An uneasy feeling snuck on me, but I couldn't find where it was coming from.

"I would rather Elisen bring it. She fought hard to get it back. It's only fitting she gets to give it to Esme."

Gregory nodded, smiling. "Oh, yes! Of course!"

I gestured to him. "Come! Let's get back to the pack. Maybe we'll meet the fighters my father had sent on our way."

Gregory seemed lost for a minute. He nodded absently. "Yes. You guys go ahead. I'll catch up with you."

Elisen and I started running in the direction of the pack. The sooner the scepter would be in a secure place, the better I'd feel.

DeMörder's POV

I watched them go with the scepter, rage filling me. I was so close to having its powers. With this power, I could have rivaled the Gods themselves. And to think only two of them could beat five of my zombies. Those incompetent fools! I needed to find a way to make them stronger or to increase their numbers even more. This wouldn't be our last encounter. Of that, I will make sure.

I had wanted to kill them ever since I found the remains of that zombie woman near my lair. One of her arms and her head had been cut off. I had tried to revive her, but I wasn't able to. I had thought my powers were stronger than this, but now I could see a limit to them. That's why I sought the power of the ceremonial scepter. I had heard great things about it and had been lucky enough to learn where it was hidden and how to get it.

The next time I meet these people, I will kill them. My body shook from the effort of the earlier race to catch up with them. I leaned on a tree. There was a wheezing sound as I took a deep breath. The black veins on my arms were darker than ever, and my skin was almost translucent. This power was taking its toll on my body, and I needed to rejuvenate myself more often.

I returned to my lair, where my disciples were waiting for me. Luckily, they had abducted two new people. The first one was a man I didn't know. I sipped his energy while my slaves held him in place. My energy slowly came back as I drank the life out of him, my skin recovering its normal appearance and my breathing returning to normal. Once the man was dead, I turned to the other man.

I burst out laughing at the sight of the person tied before me. This was the man I had grown up with. He had beaten me all those years, swearing at me, telling me I shouldn't live. All those years, he had destroyed me both physically and mentally.

My laughter echoed on the walls of the cliff surrounding me. My lips turned to an evil smile as I spoke with authority at the man on the floor, "We meet again, bastard."

The man looked at me. His face was bloody. He had been beaten, but it wasn't enough. He deserved more than this. He had tortured me for years. I would be the judge and sentence him. Then, I would execute the sentence.

His eyes widened when he saw me. "You!"

I grabbed him with one hand, pulling on his shirt. His feet didn't touch the ground, and he struggled to breathe.

"Shush now… You and I have much catching up to do tonight," I snickered.

The man managed to ask as he struggled to breathe, "How… did you… get so strong?"

I threw him to the floor. I didn't want the man to die out of lack of oxygen. That death was way too quick. He deserved something way more painful and slow than this.

He quivered from fear as I stepped closer to him. Pleasure ran through my veins at the thought of everything I would do to him. It was exhilarating, and I had to admit I was getting aroused by the idea.

"Oh, don't worry. We'll get plenty of time to chat. For you see, I won't let you die on me before the sun's rays shine."

The man tried to get away, but it was useless. I kicked him in the stomach, making him cough blood. He was still tied and couldn't stand. I grabbed his hair and brought his ear to my mouth as I whispered, "Isn't it funny how the tables turn?"

I ordered my slaves, "I will need a prisoner in case I need to draw life. I'll need a lot of energy tonight."

"Yes, master," answered Marcus.

"Oh and Marcus?"

"Yes, master?"

"I'll need to be alone for this."

"Of course, master! I will bring a prisoner, then leave you alone." He bowed his head.

The man in my hand cried at the top of his lungs, "No! Don't leave me alone! Get me out of here! Help! Someone help!"

I snickered to him, "Just as you used to tell me. Scream all you want; no one will hear you."

I brought the screaming man to my chambers. My excitement grew stronger, getting me tight in my pants as I thought about the ecstasy this night would bring.

Chapter 11 (Elisen)

Ambushed

I gave the ceremonial scepter to Esme as soon as we returned to the pack's house. I was relieved to be rid of it. She frowned when she saw the relic. She tried to cast away the dark shroud covering it but couldn't.

"A dark magic is corrupting the scepter," she commented.

She tried to cast another magic on the scepter but still to no avail.

Frustrated, she grumbled, "I don't know who cast this wicked force, but it must have been from a powerful being."

Sighing, she finally abandoned the task, "The best I can do is encase it in holy magic."

Matthew passed his arm around my hip, bringing me closer to him. The closeness of his body made me quiver. We watched in awe as Esme cast a holy cocoon over the ceremonial scepter.

When it was done, she put it in a locked chest. "It seems the scepter was safer at the pack's house after all. At least we'll know if someone tries to steal it."

We retired to our room. The night was already advanced, and I was exhausted. Our earlier plans would need to wait for another night.

"I agree," said Matthew's voice in my head.

When I turned around, he was already in bed. I cuddled against his body, listening to his breathing as I fell asleep.

The morning came too early, but I couldn't stay asleep. Matthew's blue eyes stared at me, smiling, making my heart flutter. I still couldn't believe how fast I'd fallen for him. I didn't know what love was just a few days ago, and now, I couldn't imagine my life without him.

"Morning."

I loved the sound of his deep voice. I passed my hand behind his neck, pulling his delicious mouth to mine, stealing a kiss. Matthew got on top of me. I loved his muscled body and couldn't get over how perfect he was. His lips claimed mine softly at first, but then, they devoured them with passion and need. I returned his lust, needing this physical connection as much as he did.

A slight tap came at the door, and a small voice was heard, "Mommy, daddy. Are you awake?"

I smiled at those words I never thought I'd hear. Matthew sighed, getting off me. He answered nicely, "We're awake, Molly."

She asked, "Can I come in?"

I answered, "Yes, you can come in."

The little girl opened the door, and her eyes sparkled with joy when she saw us. She ran from the door and jumped into the bed, hugging us. It would still take me time to adjust to being a mother, but I loved it.

We hugged Molly. She snuggled into our arms, whispering, "I was scared you weren't there. The man in the wall said he'd take care of you. Said you were messing with his servant too much."

The girl's words scared me. Being a soul nymph allowed her to see things others didn't, but it didn't explain everything. I had never known of any man in the wall. The fact she was seeing one scared the hell out of me. Especially since he seemed determined to kill us.

Matthew shrugged it off quickly. "Don't worry. The man in the wall can't hurt us. He's only trying to scare you."

The hairs stood up on the back of my neck. I tried to look confident, but I wasn't reassured. I had a bad feeling without knowing exactly why.

We cuddled some more, then went downstairs for breakfast.

David was there, as well as Kelly and Theo. We talked while eating breakfast. Apparently, Gregory hadn't returned to the pack's house last night. I only hoped nothing terrible had happened to him.

"I have assembled a team of ten of our best fighters," said David.

"I saw four spell casters making their way here," added Kelly.

"With a team this big, we should be able to fight the necromancer easily," said Matthew, confidence in his voice.

A cold shiver ran down my spine, and for a moment, I wondered if we should drop the fight. Necromancers were strong foes, and their magic defied death itself.

"I will always be there for you," whispered Matthew through our bond, making my heart flutter.

A thought occurred to me; the necromancer was undoubtedly the cause of the disruption of the flow of souls. I didn't know why I didn't think about it earlier, but it made perfect sense now that I had thought about it. I would need to report this to my people once we were done dealing with him.

"Let's eat quickly and go," spoke Matthew. "I want to be done with this so I can spend time with Molly and Elisen."

Matthew's voice resonated again in my mind, *"Don't worry, my love. I won't let anything happen to you."*

Through our bond, I could feel a warm, calming feeling, like a hug enveloping me.

"You will be back, won't you?" asked Molly.

I smiled at her, trying to comfort her, "Yes, Molly. We'll be back."

Matthew and I quickly dressed up for battle; we left with Kelly, Theo, and all the fighters and spell casters.

A heavy silence filled the air around us as we walked to the southwest. Everyone was lost in their thoughts. The cold hands of death passed close by, and a chill ran down my spine. I pushed through Matthew's mind, *"Please be careful."*

He pushed back, *"You as well. I don't know what I'd do if something happened to you."*

We soon got to the dead forest. The sun's rays weren't strong enough to lighten the darkness that enveloped these trees. A thick mist filled the air up to the waist. Fear crept on me; I had figured we'd already met some zombies. The fact that we hadn't only unnerved me more. Soon, a tall cliff came into view. There was only a narrow opening allowing us through.

"Everyone, stay alert," ordered Matthew as he went through first, gesturing for everyone to follow him.

Half of our group was through the opening when dozens of zombies attacked from behind.

I screamed, "Go forward! Quickly! We're being attacked!"

Kelly turned my way. "There are dozens of them ahead too! It's a trap!"

Matthew's voice echoed in my mind, *"There are too many of them. Save yourself!"*

My blood turned cold. There was no way I was leaving him here. I shouted, "Kill them! And when everyone is back, run!"

The fighters cut through the zombies, but as soon as they were dead, they would stand up again to fight. The necromancer must have been close, but I couldn't see him. The spell casters sent waves of magic and fire. Once burned to a crisp, the zombies didn't seem to revive. But waiting for them to burn was taking too long.

Kelly shouted, "Cut their heads off!"

And so we did, as many as possible, but three more appeared for every zombie we killed. It seemed they were coming endlessly.

Matthew and the others that were through finally caught back up with us. We were together, but we were surrounded. A swarm of zombies all around, black and dead. Spikes rose from the ground. I finally spotted him. On top of the cliff, I could only see the top of a crown. Anger rose in my chest. The coward, attacking from above, safe from the battle.

"Let's just concentrate on getting out of here," shouted Matthew.

We started killing zombies, slowly making our way back to the forest. A sudden sharp pain pierced me, and I had to stop, grabbing my sides with my hands. I searched for the wound but couldn't find it. A cry of agony resonated through my mind, *"Elisen."*

Something snapped, and I knew then without even looking. I turned to see Matthew's body lying on the floor. His body was intact; he had been hit by strong magic and killed instantly.

I could see his soul trying to leave his body, but the necromancer was attempting to raise him, preventing him from reaching the realm it was supposed to go, trying to make him his slave. Anger replaced the sadness that I felt. There was no way I was letting the necromancer have Matthew's soul. Kelly and Theo were closer to his body than I.

I shouted at them, "Quickly! Grab Matthew's body and bring him out of the necromancer's magic range. Hurry!"

They nodded. I started killing zombies, and the spell casters dug a path for us to flee. I could see Matthew's soul being sucked away slowly. Just when the last drop of it was about to leave, it suddenly snapped, returning to Matthew's body. I let out a breath of relief.

We were far enough, out of the necromancer's range, farther than the zombies. We kept running as fast as we could. When we were long past the dead forest, back into the normal outskirts of the pack's territory, we stopped.

Kelly and Theo laid Matthew's body on the floor, catching their breaths. Although I was glad the necromancer hadn't stolen his soul, a wave of sadness hit me, ripping me inside, hurting like nothing I'd ever felt. His soul was now leaving his body as it was supposed to, softly joining the soul flow. It would need to be judged before deciding where it should go in the afterlife.

Hot tears rolled down my cheeks as I screamed my pain. Nothing I could do would make it go away. My life felt empty. I had lost my soulmate and my only love. Molly's face came to mind, thinking she had now lost three parents. How could a child go through this and live normally? To think he had saved me from those thugs, nursed me back to health, and taught me how to love. I wished I could have been there to save him. I had failed him.

We checked on everyone. Four warriors had died, and two spell casters were injured. I cried in silence.

Kelly put her hand on my shoulder, tears falling down her cheeks as well. "I'm sorry, Elisen. He was my best friend, but he was your mate."

Theo put his arms around her shoulders, and I felt so very alone to bear the weight of my loss.

Kelly gestured. "Come on, let's bring him back to the pack. It's too late now."

Her words resonated inside me: too late. She was right; he was dead. But… It wasn't necessarily too late!

I shouted at her, "Go on, bring his body to the pack's house, but don't bury him yet."

I started running north. Kelly asked, "What are you doing?"

"I'm a soul nymph. I'll get his soul. Take care of his body until I come back."

I turned and ran. Time was running short. I had to hurry if I was to make it before his soul left.

Serena's POV

I sat in the grass at the forest's edge, watching the darkness engulf the light as the sun set on the horizon. I loved the beautiful light show that occurred at night; fireflies and fairies flying through the grass, creating a whimsical display of light. I sometimes spent hours admiring their beauty before getting back to the pack. It was a welcomed distraction from everything that was happening. With people going missing to the theft of the ceremonial scepter, it was hard to find peace of mind. With a flick of the wrist, I lit a flame in my hand.

I walked back to the pack. Charles was standing beside the wall, guarding the pack's house.

I smiled at him. "Hi, Charles."

He straightened up at the sound of my voice, staring at me with his green eyes.

"Hi, Serena. Back from enjoying the sunset?"

"You know me."

Charles smiled and replaced a fallen strand of hair behind my ear, his hand slightly brushing against my cheek.

"You know I have always loved your jet-black hair."

"I know. You always said it reminded you of the night."

He smirked. "And you know how I always enjoy the night. And your blue eyes sparkle like bright sapphires."

Charles was a good friend. He was a werewolf. I knew he had a crush on me, but I always saw him only as a friend. I tried to be nice to him. He never asked me on a date, and I hoped he never would. Or else, I'd have no choice but to turn him down, and I didn't want to hurt his feelings. So, even though it was apparent, I was playing innocent and ignored his attempts to flirt with me.

I laughed. "Yes, I know."

Just as I was about to go, a growl was heard. Beside us stood a decaying corpse. The woman was limping badly on one leg, and I wondered how she could stand.

"Stand back!" shouted Charles protectively.

I smiled. He was an amazing guard.

"Let me help."

Charles glanced at me, then nodded. I cast fire on the zombie while he attacked her with a sword. The zombie didn't seem to mind Charles's stabbing. She kept getting up and hitting him, despite being stabbed multiple times. Annoyed, I summoned a blaze on the zombie. Her whole body burst into flames, the smell of roasted skin filling the air. We watched as she slowly burned, the zombie being more erratic in her movements. Her cry finally stopped, and her body crumbled to the ground. I waited, but the zombie didn't rise again. It was all black and charred.

"What's a zombie doing inside the pack's territory?" asked Charles in shock.

I shook my head. "I don't know, but we must find a solution to this zombie problem soon."

Charles nodded, and I took my leave.

On my way to my room, I heard whispers from the Alpha's room. With the move coming, the strategic meetings didn't seem to end. David stayed up all night, talking with the advisors and ensuring everything was ready. Only a few days now. I was nervous about leaving the place where I grew up.

Odilia and Garry played with Molly while her adoptive parents were gone. Odilia seemed to be having a perfect time with the little girl. I refrained from laughing at Garry, who struggled to hold the small cup of tea the child had given him. I smiled, thinking how good of parents they would be when Odilia's child was born.

Just as I was about to go up the stairs, Kelly and Theo returned, holding Matthew in their arms.

"Make way!" they shouted.

Alpha David stormed out of the room to see his son.

"Is he injured?" he inquired.

Kelly was about to answer something, but seeing Molly staring, she revised herself, "He's only sleeping, my Alpha."

David frowned and came to check on his pulse.

Molly asked in a small voice, "Can I hug him?"

Sensing something was wrong, Odilia stopped her. "Let him sleep, sweetheart. You'll see him when he wakes up."

The little girl studied Matthew's body and frowned but said nothing. Then she asked, "Where's Mommy?"

Kelly answered, "She's gone into the woods. She needs to get something important."

David frowned again. "Odilia, Garry. Could you get Molly into bed while I talk with Kelly?"

They nodded, and Garry answered, bowing his head slightly, "Of course, Alpha."

Odilia took Molly in her arms, and the little girl's haunting gray eyes studied me, filled with worry, over Odilia's shoulder as she continued down the hallway.

When they were out of the room, David angrily asked, "What the hell happened to my son?"

Theo answered, "We were ambushed, sir. He's…"

He couldn't finish his sentence, but Kelly said it for him, "dead."

My heart was crushed at those words. Matthew was a good friend, and I was looking forward to the day he'd become the next Alpha. He was the Alpha's son, for God's sake! If he couldn't defeat the necromancer, I didn't know who could.

David fell to the ground, overcome with grief.

He growled, banging his fist on the ground. "How could this be? Where is Elisen? Wasn't she his mate? Why lie to Molly?"

Kelly explained, "She said she was getting his soul back, my Alpha."

"I don't understand," barked David.

"We aren't sure either," answered Theo. "But she said it was a soul nymph thing and to care for his body until she returns. She said she'd get his soul."

David got back up and ordered, "Put him in his bed." Then he whispered, "Let's hope she succeeds. I don't know what sorcery this is, but it's my only hope."

I helped Kelly and Theo put Matthew in his bed. It was heartbreaking to see him so lifeless and cold. I reached my room and didn't even bother to turn the light on. Exhausted and overwhelmed, I cried until slumber took me over.

I woke up. It was still dark. Strangely, I didn't feel tired anymore. I got up and checked the clock. Eight o'clock. That's strange. The sun should have been up for a long time now. I put on a pair of jeans and a shirt and got downstairs.

Everyone was in the kitchen, talking. Odilia hugged Molly in her arms, and Garry stood by their side. You could feel the tension in the air; people were scared.

"What the hell is going on?"

"That's impossible!"

"What should I tell the children?"

No one had any answers. Everyone voiced their concerns out loud, hoping someone would help them. The Alpha stood in the middle of everyone. He looked tired. His brown hair was messy, and it looked like he hadn't shaved in days, but he stood tall, listening to everyone's worries. With the missing people, the necromancer, the death of his son, and now this, I wondered how he could still stand. I guess it was true what they said; only the strongest can take on the role of the Alpha. It wasn't just about physical strength but also emotional and mental strength.

Esme entered the room. Her back was stooped with the weight of years, but she remained strong. People respected her as much as they respected the Alpha.

The Alpha's voice was deep and strong, imposing respect as he spoke, "Esme, do you have any idea what's going on?"

The room went silent, waiting for the witch's answer. She stared at him with her mysterious gray eyes.

"I have consulted every history book. Nothing like this has ever been seen in the history of our people."

The room went silent. Molly slowly walked to Esme. "I think I know why."

I held my breath at those words. Esme asked the child gently, "Really. Will you tell me?"

The child nodded shyly. "The man in the wall was laughing. He said he finally got Hemera, but I don't know who it is."

Esme's eyes opened wide. The Alpha had a stern look on his face. Hemera was the Goddess of the day, but I didn't remember everything from my history classes. It had been so many years since I'd finished school. I was now twenty-six years old. But at least I knew the name of my gods and goddesses. Hemera played a vital role in our lives.

The Alpha answered, "Yes, it makes sense."

There were murmurs in the room. People started asking questions.

"What are we going to do?"

"What about our crops?"

"Should we cast an artificial sun?" asked one of the witches.

"Why would the Goddess of the day do this?" asked a young werewolf. "Aren't goddesses supposed to be nice?"

"That's what we need to figure out," answered the Alpha.

"But what does this have to do with the sun being still out?" asked another.

Esme walked to the Alpha's side. She was so small compared to him.

"Don't you remember? Nyx, the Goddess of the night, and Erebus, the demon of darkness, bring the night upon us every night. Erebus's dark mist encircles the world and fills the deep hollows of the earth. In the evening, Nyx, his wife, draws Erebus's darkness across the sky, bringing the night. In the morning, their daughter, Hemera, the Goddess of the Day, emerges from her cave palace in the Underworld and forces Nyx and Erebus back into their home to return the day."

"Something must be preventing her from returning the day to us," I whispered.

"Exactly!" Esme said as she nodded.

"What should we do?" asked a witch.

"We will send someone to investigate," said the Alpha in a firm voice.

The room went silent. The Alpha pointed at me.

"Serena, you will go!"

"Me?" I asked in disbelief.

David nodded.

"You're one of our best spell casters. I'm sure you'll be able to find out what happened to Hemera."

"Who will come with me?" I asked.

"I'm afraid that with our current… issues, we can't spare other members of the pack to go with you."

I gasped at his words. I was to go alone? This seemed dangerous. What if I met zombies on my way?

"I have faith in you. It is only a reconnaissance mission. You find out what happened, then come back and tell us, and we'll act on it as a pack. You'll be stealthier if you go alone."

I nodded. It's not like I had a choice; the Alpha had given his order. Being stealthy was one of my strong points. I could conceal myself with magic if needed.

"All right. Does anyone have an idea where I should start?" I asked.

Esme nodded.

"There is a shrine dedicated to Hemera to the southeast. I'll show you on a map."

She gestured for me to follow her. Together with the Alpha, we walked to the war-thinking room. The big map was still hanging on the wall. She pointed to the South, further than the pack's territory.

"There. That's where the shrine is located."

I had a good idea of how to get there. It shouldn't be too difficult. It would probably take me a few hours.

"Alright, I guess I'll leave right away, then."

The Alpha put his strong hands on my shoulders.

"Thank you, Serena. I have faith in you. Come back as soon as you find out."

I nodded to him.

"Of course, Alpha."

He smiled at me.

"You know you can call me David."

I smiled. We weren't supposed to call the Alpha by his first name. But David was one of my parent's best friends. I was raised calling him an uncle, even though we weren't related. I loved him like family.

"Of course, but I always make sure to pay my respects."

"Believe me. My wolf knows you respect him. I love you as if you were my daughter."

I smiled at his words. He hugged me before adding, "Come back safely, sunflower."

Since childhood, he had always called me like that; sunflowers were my favorites. I loved the tragic story of Clytie and Apollo. I loved how sunflowers followed the sun-like Clytie longed for Apollo's love. My mother had bought me sunflower seeds. She would insist that they bring good fortune and vitality. I had set up my own little sunflower field. I would spend all of my time there. Ever since David had given me this nickname. As I exited the pack's house, I was saddened to see the sunflowers facing east, waiting for the sun's rays to hit them. They would wait forever, just as Apollo never returned Clytie's love before she was turned into a sunflower. A feeling of pride overtook me, as it was now my job to ensure that the sun returned to the flowers.

I headed southeast. It was weird to think that it was supposed to be the day. I should have heard the birds singing in the trees. Instead, the frogs and crickets were singing. A warm summer breeze caressed my skin. I was happy that it was summer. The night still felt warm. I made my way through the woods. I didn't know this part of the forest, as it was beyond the pack's territory. But I was used to following the stars. I was lucky that there were no clouds in the sky.

A sound startled me a few feet away from me. I hoped I wouldn't stumble on zombies again. The trees were dense at this spot, so I couldn't see clearly what it was. I could barely make up the shape of a man bent over something, but I couldn't see what it was.

I summoned a small flame in my hand to see better. I held back a scream when I realized that the man before me was feeding from a dead deer. Bile rose in my mouth, but I swallowed it, not wanting to draw unnecessary attention. It took a moment for me to realize that the man wasn't eating the animal; he was drinking its blood; he was a vampire. Panic filled me at this realization. Vampires were dangerous and wild. I needed to get away while he hadn't noticed me, but I wasn't sure how to do so. Holding my breath, I put out the flame in my hand. Just as I did, the vampire turned his head my way, his yellow eyes faintly glowing in the night. There was no point in hiding now. He had seen me. Vampires were so fast; it was useless for me to run, but I started to run anyway. I immediately heard a twig snap under the weight of the corpse of the deer falling.

I only took a few leaps before he caught me. I squealed when his arms pinned me against a tree. He was tall and strong. There was no way I could escape him. He had short brown hair and a trimmed beard. Blood still dripped on his chin as he studied me with his yellowish eyes. Tears began to fall down my cheeks as I was so scared.

My chin trembled as I asked with a small voice, "Please, don't kill me."

The vampire studied me. I shuddered when he got closer, taking in my scent.

"I can smell magic. You're a witch."

I nodded my head nervously.

"Are you responsible for the darkness surrounding us?"

I shook my head. He added in his deep voice, "How can I know that you're not lying?"

My eyes went wide. I stared at him, not knowing what to answer.

He frowned. "Has your tongue been cut out? Can't you speak?"

I stuttered, "I… I was sent by my pack… to investigate t-the cause of the darkness."

He studied me more. I waited anxiously. It seemed as if he was assessing whether or not he could trust me. His face came close to mine, breathing in my scent, the tip of his nose barely touching my neck, and I let out a slight cry of fear that he might drink my blood. Finally, he pulled back, his face softened, and his lips curled up. He wiped the blood from his face with the back of his hand.

"Fine. Maybe we can investigate together. I was also sent by the vampire Lord to investigate what's happening."

He released the hold he had on me and offered me his hand. His change of attitude was sudden, but I preferred this attitude more than the way he was just before. I stared at his hand, hesitating. I was still wary of him.

"Come," he said once more. "You'll be safer with me than alone."

The way he said it, it was more of an order than a choice. With the strength he possessed, he could have killed me easily. I guess that he didn't intend to do so, or it would be done already.

I didn't know what waited for me at the shrine. My magic alone wouldn't be enough if I had to fight a creature. I guess it was true; I was safer with him than alone. I smiled slightly as I grabbed his hand. It was cool to the touch. I had never been close to a vampire before.

Something sparked inside me as he smiled again. This time, he looked friendly.

"I'm Jasper. I'm a guard at the vampire Lord's castle."

I looked up into his eyes. They were still glowing lightly in the dark, but I could see some brown mixed with the yellow of his iris.

"I'm Serena. I'm a witch from David's pack."

We walked together toward the South.

"You keep saying pack, but I don't sense any wolf in you."

I nodded.

"It's true. Our pack consists of werewolves and witches. I wasn't born with a wolf, but some are."

A slight growl escaped his chest, reminding me that vampires and werewolves were sworn enemies. I considered myself lucky. If I had been a werewolf, he probably would have killed me on sight. Although he didn't like werewolves, he kept a straight face and hid it as he spoke.

"That's interesting. I've never heard of a pack of witches and werewolves. I'd love to learn more about it. Where were you headed?"

I looked at him. I was still wary of him but trusted him enough to tell him where I was headed. Somehow, I knew he wouldn't hurt me. My heart was still beating faster than usual, but I was starting to relax.

"To the southeast, there is a shrine dedicated to Hemera, the Goddess of the day."

He nodded. "That's a better idea than what I was doing."

I asked, curious, "And what were you doing?"

He chuckled. "Flying and running aimlessly, hoping to find a clue about what's happening."

I laughed at his statement. "It's a good thing you found me, then."

"Yes, you were the light I was looking for."

I was glad it was night, so he couldn't see the pink that rose to my cheeks at his comment.

Chapter 12 (DeMörder)

A pure race

I clenched my fists, my hands shaking. Adrenaline was rushing through my veins. There was a pounding in my ears as I watched them drag the dead werewolf away from my powers' range. I was so close to having my revenge on him! He was strong; I'm sure he would have made a strong zombie. At last, he was dead, one less thorn in my side.

Now that my lair had been found, I had been exposed. I needed to prepare for an attack. At least, this morning, the sun didn't rise. That only meant that the demon was getting stronger. It also meant that I was meeting my part of our bargain. He had asked that I kill as many as possible, which I did. I wouldn't want to face his wrath. And if he was happy with my deeds, he might grant me more power. Thinking about what I could do if I were more powerful made me long for more.

I returned to my throne. Judah and Marcus were there, standing by, as usual. I stared at Judah's hard traits. I still remember the day I first met him.

I had held a knife against his throat. He had fought well but imbued with dark magic, I had won. Sweat beaded on my forehead. Still, he wasn't pleading for his life. I remember how he spat at me, teeth gritted. "Go ahead. Do it."

His words were new and refreshing.

I snickered, "Are you so eager to die?"

He sneered uncannily. His eyes stared into mine, lifeless. That's when I realized he had died long ago and was now only a hollow shell.

He replied, "There's nothing for me here, anyway."

Something clicked in my head.

"You and I are similar."

The man replied, annoyed, "If I were like you, I wouldn't be lying on the ground. I would have power, as you do."

I froze. I understood precisely how he felt, as I had felt the same way when I met the demon. Was it pity or a strange connection I felt with the man?

Nonetheless, I felt compelled to make an offer to him, "Then side with me. Die by my hand, or live to serve me. Be the vessel of my vengeance. Kill in my name. Raise my army. You will have the power you want when I am a king."

A thick silence filled the air between us. He finally nodded. "Fine, I accept. I've killed countless times. Killing more doesn't scare me."

I got off him and helped him stand. In his eyes laid the despair of a man who had lost everything. A shiver ran down my spine. Nothing was more deadly than a man who had nothing to lose.

"What's your name?" I asked.

The man bowed his head to me. "Judah."

"Welcome to my ranks, Judah. We have a lot to do."

He stared into my eyes, a strange energy glowing into them. "Your words are my orders, master."

I stood from my throne.

"Judah, Marcus. Get everyone. I have an announcement to make."

They bowed. "Yes, Harvester of death."

I waited as zombies and worshippers started assembling in front of me. They barely fit in the area anymore. There were now thousands of them. The forest had been long dead, and my dark force spread even further. The time to hide was over.

Now, I had already taken my revenge on my tormentor. It had been deliciously wicked, and I enjoyed every moment of it. Just thinking about it again made my cock twitch. Now was the time to take my revenge on the people who called themselves my family. The ones who laughed at me for years while pretending to be nice.

I stood from my throne. My worshippers were there, waiting for my orders. There were so many of them that I couldn't see the end of the crowd. They spread all the way to the entrance of the cliff. Despite being so many of them, silence reigned. I would guide them like the messiah I was.

I spoke loudly, my voice echoing on the cliff's walls, "Rejoice! Today, we march to the northeast. We kill all who oppose us and destroy everything on our path. Our time has come!"

The zombies stayed motionless while the worshippers raised their arms in the air. "All hail to the Harvester of death!"

Judah walked up to me. "Finally. I will give my life for you, Harvester of death."

I ordered them forth, Judah walking beside me as my general. I felt energized as we started marching out in the fields. This would be a grand day, the day we changed history forever.

Elisen's POV

As I ran through the forest, I caught sight of Gregory. He had a weird look and was walking toward the pack. There was a lot of noise nearby, but I didn't have time to ask what was happening. I needed to hurry. I wanted to get to Matthew's soul before it went into the afterlife. I soon came across a small human town. This was the area I had been caught by thugs earlier. Although I knew that not all humans were bad, I also knew they feared what they didn't understand. And so, I took a detour to the east to ensure I didn't encounter anyone.

Soon, I could see the waters of the St-Lawrence river. Its waters were clean and strong: a natural protection for my people's domain. The waters were powerful enough that you couldn't cross on foot. The crystal shard embedded in my forearm glowed. It resonated with the crystals growing on our realm's island. We didn't understand why exactly, but all soul nymphs were born with one, as if the magic of the crystals was linked to us as we came into existence from the soul realm. For a moment, my thoughts went to Molly. She wasn't born on the island, but she was born from a soul nymph's mother. Did she also have a crystal embedded? I'll have to check when it's all over. And bring her here, so she can learn about her heritage and people.

As I concentrated on the crystal in my arm, it started emitting a warm glow. The island's crystals shone at the same frequency, and they began growing, entangling themselves until they formed a bridge of woven blueish crystals. I crossed the river onto the island. When I had crossed, I concentrated on the crystal again, and the bridge shattered, crystal dust spreading through the river's waters, giving the riverbed a glow despite the night.

I walked through the crystals and glowing mushrooms. A luscious forest grew on the island, but this was the only place I had ever seen crystals and mushrooms like these. The portal revealing my people's domain lit up as I grew closer, letting me in.

I immediately felt at home when I entered the soul nymph's realm. My friend Elysia rushed to see me; her light purple hair was beautifully braided to the right side of her face. Her ice-blue eyes shine with joy. She was one of the border guards. She was tasked with monitoring every soul crossing our realm's frontier. Not that humans or werewolves could cross, but some ethereal creatures sometimes crossed and wreaked havoc.

"Elisen!" she exclaimed as she hugged me. "I thought you'd never come back! I was so worried!"

I hugged her, the warmth of her friendship radiating through my chest.

"Elysia! I'm so happy to see you!"

She asked eagerly, "What happened to you? Why were you gone for so long? Have you found what's disturbing the souls' flow? I was worried about you when I saw the sun hadn't risen this morning."

All those questions needed to be answered, but time was running out.

"Oh, Elysia. I don't know why the sun hasn't risen, but I have more pressing matters. First, I need to see Delijiah. I will say everything I know."

She nodded. "Right! Of course! You need to report to her."

That wasn't the only reason I needed to see the queen, but I decided to keep it from my friend. The faster I had the soul's transport vessel, the faster I could retrieve Matthew's soul.

Elysia added, "Can I come too?"

I smiled at her. "Of course!"

As we ran together, I smiled at how our domain hadn't changed since I left. Soul nymphs bathing in the glowing waters of the rivers surrounding the mosh valleys. Enormous willow trees with their leaves dancing in the wind. Far away, I could see the souls pouring into the mist pool. This was the waiting area. The judges were sitting in their house. Once in a while, one would come out, fishing one soul from the pool and bringing it inside the house. They would recall the soul's past life and then decide together on the soul's fate. This was a long and arduous task, and I only hoped that Matthew's soul was still there. A knot formed in my stomach at the thought of me being too late. How could I ever think of living without him?

Finally, I could see Delijiah from far away. She was standing in her long pink dress. Her white hair was up in her usual bun. She was giving orders to other soul nymphs and instructing the young ones.

"My queen," I said solemnly.

"Ah, Elisen. You're finally back." She smiled.

"Yes, I've come to give my report."

I related everything to her while Elysia was listening closely. They shivered in fear when I recounted how I had been taken hostage by those thugs, almost dying of thirst and hunger. Then I told them how a group of werewolves and humans set me free, how they cared for me and nursed me back to health. Then I told them about the necromancer and the army of zombies.

"A necromancer!" exclaimed Delijiah with hatred. "Those foul beings are the only ones capable of disrupting the soul's flow that much. We must stop him!"

She was about to summon guards when I interrupted her, "I know how to stop him, my queen."

She raised a brow. "Is that so? How?"

I took a deep breath. "I need to borrow the soul transport vessel."

Delijah frowned. "Why would you need the soul transport vessel?"

I swallowed hard, my heart beating fast and my hands shaking. "I need to recover a soul…." I hesitated, then decided it was better to tell it all. "My fated mate's soul."

Elysia gasped at those words, then put a hand on her mouth when Delijah stared at her.

"Your fated mate?" asked Delijah coldly.

"Yes, my queen. The Moon Goddess gifted me a fated mate."

She scoffed. "That's outrageous! Soul nymphs don't have fated mates!"

"I know, my queen. But yet, I have met him. He saved my life. And now, I must save his soul."

She pressed her lips together, staring at me sternly. "Do you… love him?"

I nodded and bit my lower lip. "Yes. I love him. And I can't imagine living without him."

Her cheeks turned red. Her words were cold as ice, "Soul nymphs don't love, Elisen. We are a pure race. We don't get involved in these lows. You should have known better."

"But why?" I asked. "Why is it wrong to love?"

She came closer, her face only inches from mine, spitting her words with disdain, "Soul nymphs are a pure race, born from the chaos of the soul realm. We do not dwell on meaningless feelings like love. Yet, once in a while, it seems one soul nymph always gets tainted with feelings like this… It only plays with your judgment. Clearly, yours has been wronged too. Truly disgusting."

"Please, my queen. I need to save him."

She turned away from me. Looking at Elysia, she spoke with authority, "Take her away. She's been tainted. It's a pity." She gestured with her hand, hate seeping into her voice, "Lock her in the spirit cell."

Elysia bowed to the queen. "Yes, my queen."

Elysia looked at me sadly, grabbing my arms and locking them with magical handcuffs as she whispered, "I'm sorry. I must follow the orders."

Panic rose in me. I couldn't go to the spirit cell. They use it for the dissident nymphs who broke the rules and committed crimes, like this nymph, who used to take good souls and send them to the Underworld for fun. Or those who allowed the worst murderous souls into the Elysian plains. But I had done nothing! I didn't deserve to go there.

They didn't physically restrain you; they controlled your spirit. The Rialtóir was in charge of mind-controlling the prisoners. It was a giant furry creature with a black head like a cat, two golden feathered wings, and paws like a fox. The beast had been created by Psyche and Hypnos. It had been given to the soul nymphs as a reward for their hard work. The creature was friendly, and young soul nymphs usually cuddled in his fur. I used to play with it all the time as a child. Never had I imagined I'd fear this creature.

I could already see the Rialtóir with dozens of nymphs standing, mouth agape, staring at the void. They were under his control. There was no need to restrain them. They would stay there, standing for eternity, living in a dream forever. No one knew what they were seeing, and I didn't want to find out.

"Elysia, please. I'm your friend. Don't do this."

She bit her lower lip. "Is it true what you said? Did you really fall in love with this man?"

"He's a werewolf. And yes, I fell in love with him."

"But soul nymphs don't fall in love. I've never felt anything like that."

"I know. But I didn't choose this!"

She frowned. "How could you not have chosen this?"

"You don't choose to love someone. It just happens from within your heart and your soul."

Elysia had a pensive look for a while. It seemed unfair to be sentenced to prison for something that wasn't my fault.

"What does it do?" whispered Elysia.

"What?"

"To love someone."

I thought for a moment. Describing love was hard, especially since it was new to me.

"It's an amazing feeling, Elysia. To care for someone like you had never done before. So much more than friendship. To want to be there for them, to give up on everything. Like they become the most important person to you. And when they love you back, your heart beats strongly. It's like the greatest gift you could ever be given."

Elysia took in what I said, smiling. "It sounds wonderful."

"It is! And it's not fair that I get punished for feeling this."

She looked away as we continued to walk. I was getting too close to the Rialtóir to my liking. I needed to get away, and fast! Suddenly, Elysia stopped. "Why do you need the soul transport vessel?"

I stared into her eyes. "Matthew was killed by the necromancer. We were fighting with him. I must recover and return his soul to his body before it's too late."

She looked at me in surprise. "You're fighting the necromancer?"

I nodded. "Yes, we are!"

She looked at the Rialtóir, then stared at me. "I'll be in big trouble for this."

My heart hammered in my chest at her words. "Say it was my fault. That I attacked you and ran away."

She nodded, then removed my handcuffs, whispering, "Run! Hurry, my friend. Get him back."

Tears rolled down my cheeks. "Thank you so much, Elysia."

She smiled and waved as I ran as fast as I could toward the palace.

The queen's palace soon came into view. It was on the top of a hill. Massive stone stairs led to it. At the castle's base were pillars of crystal and gold and massive arches decorated with golden leaves. The second floor was more massive than the first floor, with a terrasse on the roof mounted by gold towers at each corner. Multiple pearl-white round statues decorated with delicate gold thread patterns stood in a row near the castle. We called them the Goddess's tears. No one knew what they were made of, but they represented purity and the divine task our race had been given: to carry souls to their afterlife.

I stuck to the shadows as much as possible, trying to avoid being spotted by the guards. When I got close enough to the castle, I wondered how to sneak in. Guards were stationed at each entry, and there was no way to get in without being seen. I could still see the queen in the fields giving orders. This was perfect, as she wouldn't be inside the castle. I didn't see any panic or movement in the guards. This meant the queen was unaware I wasn't in the spirit cell. I needed to use this to my advantage.

I went up the stairs by one of the secondary entries of the castle. The one on the far right side of it. One of the guards on duty was Carleon. He was one of my good friends and one of the only males of our race. No one understood why, but since we no longer reproduced, almost all soul nymphs were women. The evolution of the race had decided on this. But some speculated that for a male to be born, the soul had to be submitted to different levels of magic or receive magic from a different God or Goddess before birth. Others simply thought that the soul realm had changed over the centuries and that the conditions required for male soul nymphs weren't met anymore.

I didn't know the other guard. She was tall and muscular, and I hoped Carleon would let me in. I walked casually to them.

"Hi, Carleon! I'm so glad to see you!"

He smiled as I approached, his yellow eyes full of joy at my sight.

"Elisen! I had yet to hear you were back! How was the investigation?"

An idea popped into my mind. "That went well! And I found the source of the disruption to the soul's flow!"

His eyes widened. "Really? What is it?"

I smiled, forging a lie that would grant me entrance to the palace, "Oh, just a really big sielûnn blocking the flow of the river of souls."

Carleon was surprised. "Really? They don't usually get out of the soul realm."

Sielûnn were ethereal creatures that devoured souls. Their skin was gray, and they had wings. They stood on their back legs, and had a long tail. Their eyes glowed turquoise in the dark. They were usually relatively small, not more than three feet tall. Carleon was right; they didn't usually get out of our realm, as it was easier for them to feast on souls here. But I needed my lie to sound believable.

"I know! I was surprised too! But this one is way bigger than usual! He found a place where the soul river flows outside our domain. From the look of it, he's been eating way more than he should."

Both guards chuckled at my last sentence. I continued, "Anyway, I need to borrow the soul transport vessel."

Carleon asked, "Why?"

"Well, since it's too big for me to chase it as usual, I'll pick him up in the soul transport vessel and put him back where he belongs."

Carleon frowned and thought for a moment.

"Hum… It's true that the soul transport vessel can also transport ethereal creatures. That's actually a good idea. Do you think he will fit in it?"

I nodded. "Don't forget that ethereal creatures can change shape and size when sucked into a device."

He grinned. "Right! I had forgotten this. Go ahead, then."

Just as I was to get inside the castle, the other guard asked, "Does the queen know about this?"

My heart skipped a beat. I grinned, trying to hide my fear of exposure. "Sure! She asked me to fetch it herself."

The other guard frowned. "Then where is her royal decree?"

"She didn't have time to make one. This is such an urgent matter that she sent me right away!"

I hoped my excuse would be good enough. The female guard narrowed her eyes at me, but Carleon nodded and spoke to her, "You can trust Elisen. I've known her for years."

The other guard examined him and me for what seemed like an eternity before finally nodding. Relieved, I hurried inside the castle before they changed their minds.

I walked down the long corridor. There were rows of marble columns on each side. They were decorated with gold designs depicting griffin wings at the top until the designs met the gold arches of the ceiling. I had never noticed before today how the castle exuded opulence. Now that I'd seen it, it disgusted me. If our race was supposed to be so pure, we didn't need that much luxury. The queen kept saying so herself.

I wondered for a minute if there was more than meets the eye about her. Everyone lived a simple life. She was the only one living in such an extravagant castle. Was she hiding something? Where had this come from? Why was she so eager to imprison me for having feelings for someone? Was loving someone making our race less pure? Was she trying to hide something?

The throne was directly in front of me, but I turned to the chamber to my left. I knew the soul transporter was in it, but I had never ventured there. Only the queen was allowed to go. I had seen her fetch it once in the past.

I was astounded by what I saw when I opened the door. The room was filled with shelves containing treasures and relics. I didn't know where these came from, but this room contained a fortune. This was shocking; why did no one know about these? I didn't have the time to figure it out. Time was running out!

I studied the shelves closely when I finally saw the soul transporter. It was shaped like a box with a rounded lid. Ancient runes engraved in gold adorned the cover. Dust and magical petals floated around the box, held in place by the magic of the transporter. I took it and walked out of the room.

As I came back to the long corridor, I heard steps. The queen was there with Carleon and the other guard. The queen's eyes widened, and her mouth opened wide when she saw me.

She screamed, "She has the soul transporter! Arrest her immediately!"

Carleon's eyes locked with mine. In them, I could read surprise, deception, and sadness. I knew I had deceived him; I had used our friendship to gain his trust. I hoped I would one day have the opportunity to explain everything to him. Maybe Elysia would tell him?

"Stay where you are!" he shouted sternly at me. "Don't make this harder than it already is."

I mouthed the word "sorry" before sprinting to the queen's room in front of me. I could hear the footsteps behind me as they tried to catch me. The queen's chamber had a large window. I grabbed a vase that was on a desk, hoping it was heavy enough, and threw it at the window. Relief filled me as the glass broke. The footsteps were getting closer. I turned back, seeing my friend's face one last time. My heart raced as I jumped through the broken window without a second thought.

Panic filled me when I realized my fall took longer than anticipated. I didn't know that this side of the hill overlooked a direct and steep cut. Pain seared through my feet up my legs as I touched the ground. I looked at the queen's head, watching me through the window. Carleon wasn't with her, and I guessed he and the other guard were now going down the stairs on the other side to run after me. I got back up, my legs were hurting, but I was uninjured. I started running toward the mist pool as fast as I could.

Chapter 13 (Serena)

First kiss

We had been walking in silence for a few hours. I heard a growl to my right. I didn't have time to check where it came from before Jasper grabbed me and pushed me to the ground to his left. I looked back up to see Jasper fighting a grizzly bear. I had no idea where it came from, but I felt grateful Jasper was there for me. The bear looked old and strong. It was on its hind legs, its front paws on Jasper's shoulders. The beast was growling violently and trying to bite him. Its jaw was dangerously close to Jasper's face. His vampiric strength allowed him to push the bear back, but I didn't know for how long. Even if the beast was dangerous, I didn't want it to die. We were probably on its territory, or maybe it was only trying to protect its babies.

I screamed at Jasper, "Don't kill it!"

He turned his head toward me while fighting. "If I don't kill it, it will kill us both."

"Wait!" I shouted.

I got up and started chanting a spell, *"Quiesco, remisi, quietus...."*

A warm wind flowed around us. I kept chanting the words. The bear stopped attacking and got back on the ground. The bear was watching me curiously. It listened for a while, hypnotized by my words, then turned around and slowly walked away.

Jasper was looking at me with a grin on his face.

"That was impressive!"

I blushed at his comment. "Thanks."

"Those powers of yours are useful! If you hadn't been there, I wouldn't have had a choice but to kill the beast."

Then I remembered how he had just saved my life.

"Thanks for saving me from the bear. How did you see it?"

He smirked. "I'm a vampire. I immediately sensed him."

He said this as if it were obvious to anyone.

"That's true, but you didn't need to protect me."

He winked. "I would have been a bad friend if I'd let it kill you."

I chuckled. "Are we friends now?"

He looked at me with a smirk. "Aren't we?"

His smirk was so handsome that I caught myself thinking that I would love to taste those lips.

I smiled at him. "I guess we are."

Jasper smiled and winked. "Then let's get going, friend."

We walked and talked for a while. I wasn't sure when I stopped being afraid of Jasper and when I started to desire his lips. All I knew was that the more I got to know him, the more I liked him. He was nice and intelligent. He was handsome, although I would never tell him. His presence made me feel safe. Somehow, my heart was still beating faster than usual, but I knew it wasn't because of fear. Being close to Jasper had this effect on me. It sounded weird; I had only met him. I was questioning my sanity at this point. Could it be that Jasper was my fated mate? I knew the Moon Goddess created an undeniable link, igniting your soul when you meet your mate, making resistance impossible. I had never experienced anything like this. I wondered what he thought of me. Was there such a thing as mates for vampires? Could he feel the pull between us? I would never dare to ask him.

Before long, the shrine to Hemera came into view. Or at least, I assumed it was that. This was the only structure we had seen, so I thought it was her shrine. A big archway framed the entrance. Four giant statues of Titans protected her shrine. They were at least twice as high as me and still in good condition. The walls of her shrine were made of rocks. In front, there was a poppy garden. The flowers were closed since it was night, but you could still tell what it was. The red of the flowers contrasted with the gray rocks from which the shrine was made.

"I guess that's it," commented Jasper.

I nodded and stayed close to Jasper as we walked inside the shrine. Pieces of the altar lingered on the floor. It was all ransacked and destroyed. All the portraits of the Goddess had been damaged. Not a single one still showed her face, but you could still see her long brown hair flowing down her hips.

Fear crept on me, my heart beating fast. What if the one responsible for this was still inside? My legs felt weak. I wanted to run away.

Jasper squeezed my hand, whispering, "It's okay. I won't let anything happen to you."

He turned to look at me while I stared at him with wide-eyed. I wondered for a moment if he knew what I was thinking. Were vampires able to do such a thing?

Right on cue, he chuckled softly. "Vampires are predators. I can smell your fear and the blood that runs through your veins."

It made sense, even though it made me uncomfortable knowing he could feel the blood pumping through my veins.

He squeezed my hand again, pulling gently on it. "Come, we must go further."

I followed him. We ventured into all the shrine rooms; each one was in the same state. We came to the farthest room. A large hole was dug in the ground. Dirt and debris were strewn about. I could see in the hole a large tunnel leading into the darkness.

Jasper whispered, "Let's go see where it leads."

He pulled on my hand, but I pulled it away and shook my head.

"No. I need to report back to the pack."

He turned toward me, his yellow eyes studying me.

"Are you serious?"

I explained, "As a pack, we act together. I was only sent to investigate what caused the darkness. I can't go alone."

Jasper came closer to me, his body almost touching mine. I had to fight against my will. All I could think of was how much I'd like to close the gap between us.

He raised my chin with a finger, making me look at him.

"You're not alone. You're with me."

I smiled. "True. But still…"

He didn't let me finish.

"Besides, we know there's a hole, and her shrine has been destroyed. It doesn't explain the darkness."

I thought for a minute. He was right. But still… "I would feel better if I had the whole pack with me."

"Wouldn't that take a day or so? What if we're not at the right place? What if this is only a distraction and the real problem is elsewhere? Shouldn't we ensure we've found this eternal night's source first?"

I pinched my lips and sighed.

"How is it that you're always right?"

He laughed heartily.

"That's the first time someone told me that. But I need to say that I agree." He grinned, rubbing the back of his head. "You'd better remember that I'm always right."

I laughed too. There was no way I could keep a straight face.

He didn't wait for an answer and gestured. "Come."

He put his hand down my back, gently pushing me forward. The way he touched me made my heart flutter in my chest. There was a connection between us. One that was deeper than anything I'd felt before. The only plausible explanation was that he was my mate, even if he was a vampire. This went against everything I had been told. Fated mates were only supposed to be possible between werewolves, witches, and humans. Or is it because werewolves and vampires were age-old enemies that they didn't mate? Did the Moon Goddess ever say there'd be no vampire mates?

I guess I'd never find out, but one question crept on me: Did he feel it too? The idea that I was the only one feeling the connection snuck in on me, eating me inside. Still, I brushed it aside and decided to enjoy the moment. I got closer to him as we walked until my shoulder touched him. I felt happy he didn't move away from me, as if it were natural. His shoulders were broader than mine, and his hand rested on my hip as we entered the tunnel.

Together, we ventured into the darkness of the hole in Hemera's shrine. Close to Jasper, I felt safe. I flicked my wrist, summoning a flame into my hand. Jasper stared at me.

"That's what I saw earlier in the woods."

I explained to him, "I can't see in the dark."

He nodded. "That's okay. Just keep it small and stay close. We don't know what lurks further."

A shiver ran down my spine at this thought.

The tunnel we were walking through became very narrow. At one point, I had to walk in front of Jasper, as it wasn't wide enough for both of us. Luckily, it became wider soon after. I briefly turned toward Jasper when sharp claws pierced through my back. I screamed from the pain, the flame in my hand extinguishing as I tried to remove the creature. Jasper moved so fast that I barely had time to see him. He pulled on the beast, yanking it off my back. Pain spread through my back as I felt the skin tearing away. I fell to the ground, my hands breaking my fall. I turned around to see Jasper fighting a winged creature. It had sharp claws and teeth, pointed ears, and bat wings. Jasper ripped off the creature's wings, making it shriek in pain. He looked like he was in a frenzy of rage. He didn't stop hitting until the creature fell to the floor and stopped moving, blood pooling on the floor. Only then did he calm himself.

He approached me, asking softly, "Are you all right?"

I winced from the pain. I could feel warm blood dripping from my back.

"What the hell was that?" I hissed in pain.

Jasper offered me his hand. "An imp. I hate those creatures."

Jasper had me turn to look at my back. He looked at me with worried eyes, his voice full of worry, "It's deep."

I smiled at him and started chanting a healing spell, "*Sano, curo, medeor.*"

Warm energy filled me, numbing the pain and making me feel better. Jasper was staring at me when I stopped chanting. I smiled at him and showed him my back.

"See? All good."

He slowly smiled, his eyes shining. "That's a relief."

I smirked. "Were you actually worried about me?"

He hesitated for a moment. "I was."

I froze at those words. I wasn't expecting his answer. My heart skipped a beat at the thought that he was concerned for me.

He added, "I thought you were going to die."

He closed the distance between us, his strong hands gently caressing my arms. I stared at those arms that had crushed the imp so easily. Yet they were gentle with me, and I felt safe around them. I leaned into his embrace, my lips almost touching his.

I whispered, "I'm not dying anytime soon."

His lips brushed against mine as he whispered, "I'll make sure of it."

As soon as he said those words, his lips were on mine, a moan escaping my lips as we kissed. His kiss was possessive as if he had held back for so long and finally allowed what he longed for. He was my long-awaited rain after a long drought, and I drank every drop of him. At this moment, I knew this was meant to be, and I never wanted it to end. Unspoken words flew around us, my hands roaming his muscled chest. My heart was hammering in my chest as Jasper wrapped his arms around my hips, pulling me closer to him.

I was panting when we broke the kiss. Catching my breath, I stared at him, still wrapped in his arms, surrounded by his manly scent. An awkward silence filled the space between us. This had been so sudden. Our hearts were expressing what our minds had yet to grasp.

He spoke with hesitation.

"I… don't know what came over me. I'm sorry."

He looked like he felt bad about kissing me, and I didn't want him to feel like that. I had yearned for this so much!

I answered, "Don't feel sorry. I wanted this."

His eyes lit up at those words, but I could still see the doubt in them.

"Are you sure? You know that I'm a vampire. Aren't you scared of me?"

I shook my head, letting my fingers roam over his chest absentmindedly.

"We might be different, but I'll learn to know you. Besides… I can't argue with the Moon Goddess."

Jasper had a curious look on his face.

"The Moon Goddess? What do you mean?"

I explained, "My people speak of fated mates. Someone made especially for you, decided by the Moon Goddess herself."

Jasper caressed my cheek with the back of his hand as he answered.

"My people also speak of fated mates. Although, I thought it was only a legend."

I stared into his eyes, seeing his soul.

He continued, smiling as he spoke, "Yet, I feel a connection with you. Deeper than anything I have felt before. Something I have never thought possible. I've never been so scared as when I thought you would die. A rage filled me. I would have destroyed anything if it meant saving you."

I could feel his sadness and anger as he spoke. I put my hand on his chest.

"But I'm fine. I'm here, thanks to you."

He calmed down immediately.

He asked me, "You can feel it, right?"

I nodded. "I do. And I will feel your emotions more as our bond increases. That's how fated mates work. They even say mates can communicate by thought."

He smiled, his hands grabbing my hips firmly.

"I guess fated mates are true, then."

I kissed him once more, my tongue dancing with his. I could never grow tired of tasting him. He rested his forehead on mine, staring deeply into my eyes.

"You're the best thing that ever happened to me," he breathed.

My heart beat strong at his words. All I wanted to do was to stay in his arms.

"I want to love you for the rest of my life," I whispered.

He squeezed me lovingly, but being in this dark tunnel brought me back to reality. "Maybe we should get going?"

He chuckled at my question. "I guess we still need to solve this mystery."

I nodded. Together, fingers intertwined, we ventured forward.

Elisen's POV

My lungs hurt, but I kept running. I didn't hear anyone behind me but didn't dare look back. What mattered was that I got to the mist pool before Matthew's soul disappeared. Finally, the judges' house was in sight. It was next to the pool of souls, with a long balcony and a turret. No one knew precisely what the turret was for, and no one ever ventured up to it, but it was beautiful and gave the house a grand look. Mist permeated the air and covered the pool, but I knew it was there, beside the willow tree.

I was now close enough to see the souls wandering the mist pool, waiting for the judges to come. There were dozens of them, just walking aimlessly. I had never been that close to the mist pool before. As a soul nymph, I was never involved in judging the souls. I was only to guide them to the afterlife. Seeing it was surreal.

As I got closer, the bond pulled on me. It was weak at first but got stronger as I kept walking. My heartbeat quickened, and I got butterflies in my stomach. This meant that his soul was still there. I had to find him. I searched through the souls as I whispered softly in a trembling voice, "Matthew?"

Our most important task was assisting the judges, so I knew they were nearby. I knew I couldn't afford to speak too loudly. I wouldn't want to attract the attention of the judges or of the soul nymphs working with them.

Suddenly, I heard a faint and distant whisper in my mind, "Elisen."

My mind focused on him, our bond pulling at me, and I suddenly saw him. He was walking toward the afterlife door, guided by one of us. I couldn't let this happen. I was willing to risk everything for him.

I sprinted toward him, screaming as loudly as possible, "No, Matthew! Don't go!"

As I got closer, Matthew's soul started to glow. The closer I got, the brighter it got. Even the nymph accompanying him was staring in surprise. When I finally got to him, he glowed so brightly that it was hard to look at him. In my mind, I heard him speak only one word, "Mate." I could feel all his love and happiness through this only word, as if it was the most important word ever.

"What's happening?" asked the nymph, stunned.

I smiled at her. "He's my soulmate."

She was still standing there, frozen by surprise. I held out the vessel of souls to Matthew, whispering, "You need to get in there. Don't worry. Soon, we will be reunited."

The soul nymph looked at the soul transport, amazed, "You have the transport vessel?"

I nodded to her and pointed to Matthew's soul. "Yes. I'm taking him with me."

She stared in awe, unsure of what to do. I gestured to Matthew. He didn't answer anything but nodded knowingly. His soul soon disappeared into the vessel. I brought the relic against my chest. I held the most important and dearest thing in my life. I was ready to sacrifice anyone and anything standing in my way. But soon, I would be reunited with him.

I didn't wait for the nymph to process what had just happened and started running toward the edge of our realm, back to Matthew's pack.

Chapter 14 (Serena)

Underground lake

We soon arrived at a large cave. A hole in the ceiling let the light of the moon filter through. An underground lake filled the center of the room. My feet hurt from walking for hours. I had no idea what time it was. The fact that the sun didn't get up this morning didn't help. Jasper turned toward me.

"Are you feeling all right?"

"I'm just tired, I guess."

He nodded. "True. I had forgotten that humans need far more sleep than vampires."

I looked at him, surprised. "Really?"

He nodded. "I barely need a few hours of sleep to feel refreshed."

"That's not fair. I wish I could get by on a few hours of sleep daily."

He chuckled. "It's normal for you to feel tired. It's already late night."

I frowned. "How can you say that? The sun didn't even shine today."

"I can sense it."

Sensing the time of the day must be nice. Without the sunlight, I was lost and had no notion of time.

"Makes me wish I was a vampire, too."

Jasper frowned. His words were cold, "Being a vampire doesn't have all the advantages. Don't wish for something when you don't know what it entails."

I studied him. His eyes looked hurt, and I wondered what had happened in his life for him to feel this way.

"Do you wish you weren't a vampire?"

He sighed. "Some days I do… But I didn't choose this. I was born this way. Cursed, with all the hate and fighting that comes with it."

He looked back at me when I put my hand on his chest. His voice was heavy with the sadness from his past experiences. I wish he would share those with me to lighten the weight he was carrying on his shoulders.

"I don't hate you."

He smiled as he grabbed my hand, rubbing his thumb on the back of my hand.

"Then I'm the luckiest vampire on Earth."

He kissed my hand tenderly, his cool lips lingering on my skin for a moment, then added, "We'll set up camp here for the night. I'll go scout the surroundings."

Multiple tunnels extended from this room. I watched Jasper as he went in search of danger. He was so strong, yet I saw a broken heart, a vulnerable soul, just a minute ago. Someone who needed soothing and love. I couldn't even imagine the things he had to endure in his life. I was hoping to learn all about him; so that I could heal his wounded soul.

There didn't seem to be any immediate danger in the cave. I approached the lake. The moonlight and the stars reflected on it, making its water sparkle. I glimpsed at my reflection. My hair was messy, and I had dried blood on my skin and clothes.

Seeing that I was alone, I removed my clothes. The lake's waters were icy, and I held back a scream as I dipped my foot in. With the tip of my finger, I summoned a flame and heated the water until it was searing hot. Getting into the lake now felt like getting into a hot bath. I let out a breath of relief, all my muscles relaxing at the contact of the hot water. I grabbed my clothes and rinsed them in the lake. It wouldn't remove all the stains, but it was the best I could do for the moment. I put them to dry on a rock, casting a wind spell on them to make them dry faster.

While my clothes dried, I bathed in the lake. Staring at the stars, relaxing in the warm waters, and swimming softly. All my worries disappeared.

I was lost in my thoughts when I heard, "Okay, well, the surroundings look safe…."

I turned toward Jasper. He froze when he saw me.

I should have felt shy, but instead, warmth filled me. I took pleasure in Jasper's look as he saw me, realizing I was naked in the water. My breasts were still underwater, yet I smirked when I saw the bulge in his pants. I loved the power I had over his body.

I smirked at him. "Enjoying the view?"

He didn't seem sure what to answer.

"I'm sorry… I didn't know. I…"

I stopped him. My body was reacting to him the same way that his was.

"Can't you feel it?"

He looked at me as if only realizing it. I was sure he could feel what my body wanted. A purr escaped his chest, the sound lighting a fire inside me.

His eyes were lustful as he asked, "Can I join?"

I bit my lower lip as I nodded. I wanted Jasper's touch, to taste him; I wanted all of him.

He removed his clothes, letting me admire his body. I knew he was muscular, but it was the first time I laid eyes on him. His chest was large and firm. Scars scattered on his chest, showcasing the various battles he had fought. I thought he was beautiful and wanted to run my fingers along those scars. I wanted to learn everything about his body until I knew every inch of his skin. He removed his pants, revealing his hard cock. I stared at him, waiting in delight as his body entered the water. The way he sighed when he entered the water made me yearn for him even more.

"Since when are underground lakes hot?"

I smirked as I swam toward him.

"Since I heated it."

I got my hands behind his neck and wrapped my legs around his waist. He lifted me in his arms, grabbing my butt as he did. My breasts brushed on his chest.

"Gorgeous," he breathed out.

I kissed him hungrily. His touch was my undoing. His hands roamed my body, making goosebumps appear as they did. I was getting drunk off him, and I never wanted to stop.

He whispered between breaths, "I have no doubt in my mind that you're my mate."

I gasped as he proceeded to nibble my erect nipple.

I managed to answer, "And you are mine."

A purr of satisfaction escaped his chest, reverberating through me. It was a soothing, loving sound. I couldn't help but feel cherished at this moment.

He looked me deep in the eyes, asking, "Then, will you allow me to make you mine?"

I kissed his lips again, not wanting to break the heat flowing between us, my body still yearning for his as his erection pressed against me.

"How will you make me yours?"

His eyes flickered, and his canines protruded slightly from his lips. "I need to bite you and drink your blood."

I flinched at his words. I had never been bitten by a vampire, which sounded scary, but he quickly added.

"You won't feel pain. It's one of the deepest, most intimate connections we can share. I swear that you're going to love it."

I relaxed in his arms at those words. Curiosity overtook me. This intimate connection sounded great. I thrust my hips, the tip of his cock barely entering my dripping cunt, earning a grunt from him.

"All right. Let's do this," my words rolled against Jasper's neck before I licked his delicious skin, nibbling at his earlobe.

He cupped my breast, leaving a trail of kisses on my neck. I moaned as he started to rub circles on my clit, pleasure building inside me. "Say my name, love. I want to hear it on your lips."

I closed my eyes and basked in love and pleasure in a delicious moment of intimacy with the vampire I had fallen in love with. I lifted my head toward the sky, arching my back as I cried from pleasure, "Jasper!"

He grunted; his eyes were hungry with desire as I came on his finger.

"Good girl," he whispered on my lips as he devoured me, our tongues dancing together. I gasped as he entered me, my walls tightening on his hard cock. Pleasure filled me as he thrust in and out of me, carried by the lake's waves. His teeth grazed my neck. I tilted my head, pushing back my hair so he could easily access it.

"Fuck, you drive me crazy," he purred on my skin.

As he pushed harder, I dug my nails into his back, a sweet cry of pleasure escaping my lips. I pulled his head toward my neck, clearly stating I wanted him to do it. A sharp pain hit me as his canines pierced my skin, instantly replaced by a wave of ecstasy. He kept thrusting into me as he drank my blood. At this moment, I could feel his emotions, his pleasure, all of him. It was an indescribable feeling as our hearts beat in unison. My soul tangled with his in this perfect twirl, never to untangle again.

He thrust hard inside me, pushing me over the edge. My walls pulsed around him, and I couldn't help but squeal from pleasure. I didn't know how much he drank, but he removed his teeth from my neck at one point, his tongue lingering on the spot he had bitten. He kept thrusting, wave after wave of pleasure, washing over me. He grunted hard as he finally let himself come, shouting my name.

I rested my head on his shoulder and basked in the lake's warm waters, staying in this perfect moment. I heard in my mind, *"You have no idea how much I love you."*

I smiled and answered out loud, "I love you, too, Jasper."

Jasper looked at me and smiled.

"So, you can hear me."

I smiled back.

"It seems so."

"Good, then you'll never feel alone again."

I froze at the realization he had felt my most intimate thoughts. All those moments I had felt alone but didn't tell anyone about. He had seen all the feelings I didn't dare to admit, even to myself. That's how deep the mate bond went. It was scary how I couldn't hide anything from him, but neither did he. And thanks to this bond, I got to know him better than ever.

His past was filled with so much loneliness. I was glad I had found him.

"You were right," I whispered.

"About what?"

"I loved it when you drank blood from me. It was so…."

I searched for a way to describe the bliss I felt when he bit me, but words couldn't describe it.

He finished my sentence, "So perfect, right?"

I nodded as he added, "You're the sweet nectar that was made especially for me."

I breathed. "Then never let go of me."

He smiled at me.

"You're the best thing that ever happened to me. I will stay by your side forever. I would give my life for you."

I could feel the sincerity in his words as he kissed me. His beautiful eyes stared at me. My heart fluttered, and I wondered how lucky I was to have met him.

"I have known since the moment I laid eyes on you," he whispered, adding, "you should probably rest. We have a long day ahead of us tomorrow."

We got out of the lake and got dressed. I liked the fact that Jasper decided to stay shirtless. It meant that I could still admire his muscles. I summoned a fire a few feet from us to warm us up. I lay by the fire, Jasper lying beside me as he caressed my cheek.

"I never expected to find someone who made me feel this way."

This bond between us was powerful. I had never thought it'd be possible to love someone this much, this fast. It was as if my soul had known him for many lifetimes. I felt like I knew his deepest secrets, understanding him in a way no one else could.

I whispered to him, "I never expected this either."

He chuckled. "I thought fated mates were only legends."

His body felt cool against mine. It felt good and refreshing.

I confessed to him, "I never thought a vampire would be my mate."

His voice was worried as he asked, "Were you scared of me?"

I told him the truth, "I was. But I'm not anymore."

He grabbed my hand, kissing my knuckles.

"I would never hurt you. You're more precious to me than the biggest diamond. You're more beautiful than the fairest of the flowers."

My heart hammered in my chest so hard that all I could whisper back was his name.

I ran my fingers along the scars on his chest.

Concern filled his voice as he asked, "Do you think they are hideous?"

"How can you think such a thing? I want to know everything about you. I want to hear the story behind each of your scars."

A wistful smile appeared on his face.

"They are not as heroic as you think. My father was a very strict vampire. He always said that royal guards should be strong. He used to hit me and whip me every night."

I gasped at his words, horror and sadness filling my heart.

My voice trembled, "How could he do that to his son?"

His eyes stared deeply into mine as he lovingly rubbed his thumb over my bottom lip.

"Don't be sad, my love. He did it so I could learn to endure the hardships of battle. He did it until I no longer cried. My skin thickened, making me more resilient in battle."

I couldn't even comprehend how a father could be cruel to his child. I had such a loving family. The werewolves cared for each other, patiently teaching and growing the children with love.

The vampires looked very different, and I wondered if they were all like that or if Jasper was unlucky.

I kissed one of his scars.

"Then let me kiss each of these scars until I erase the memories of how they were created."

He cupped my face and kissed me lovingly, hugging me tightly and whispering, "Whatever did I do to get a mate so perfect? You should sleep. Although I don't need to rest as much as you, I'll hold you all night."

I closed my eyes and drifted to sleep, surrounded by Jasper's love.

I woke up still in Jasper's arms. He was still sleeping. I wondered what time it was since the moon was still in the sky. This night had lasted for more than twenty-four hours now. I hoped that today we'd find the cause of this. Jasper stirred in his sleep. Soon, his beautiful eyes stared lovingly at me.

I teased him, "You slept longer than me."

He smiled. "I've stayed awake, watching you sleep for hours."

"Really? And what did you do while I was sleeping?"

"Contemplating your beauty. Reminding myself that this is not a dream. Realizing how lucky I am that you were fated to be my mate. Thinking how perfect you are."

I blushed at his words and kissed him.

"I don't even know what to answer to that."

He chuckled.

"Then don't answer anything. I could feel your love yesterday when I fed from you, and I can still feel it through our bonded souls."

He was right. I could feel it too. There was no need for words, as I understood him on a level I never thought possible.

He asked, "When was the last time you ate?"

I thought for a second. "Yesterday morning."

He frowned. "Then we should go. I don't want you to starve."

I nodded. I was hungry, but I was still okay. But I couldn't spend days without eating. We needed to find food or be done with this eternal night, fast.

I looked at the multiple tunnels connecting to this cave, wondering which one to take.

Jasper commented as he put his shirt back on, "They all come to a dead end except this one to the left. That's the only one I had to watch while you slept."

"Then we know which way to go."

He grabbed my hand, intertwining his fingers with mine as we walked toward the tunnel he had pointed to.

Chapter 15 (Matthew)

The queen's downfall

My eyelids felt heavy, and I had a pounding head-ache. All the muscles in my body ached. My mind felt foggy. I faintly remember Elisen call-ing my name as if in a dream. I could hear whispers around me and smell her delicious scent.

"Mate!" my wolf spoke in my mind.

She was there. All I wanted to do was hold her in my arms, but I couldn't move.

"Please, open your eyes," Elisen's sweet voice echoed in my mind. It was full of worry, and I wondered what had happened. The last thing I remember was the ambush with the zombies. We were fighting them, surrounded, killing one after the other, and then, it went blank.

I listened but heard no fighting. No wind blew on my skin, and I could swear we were back at the pack's house. What the hell had happened?

I tried to open my eyes, but my body didn't obey. I kept trying, and after a few tries, I finally opened them. I stared at the ceiling, my head felt too heavy to move around, but I could feel my strength returning. The Alpha blood in me would surely heal whatever had happened to me in no time.

"He opened his eyes!" Molly's small voice exclaimed happily.

She hugged me tightly, squeezing as much as she could.

"Careful," spoke Elisen, "don't squeeze too tight."

I managed to curl my lip up, passing my arm around my little girl and hugging her back.

Molly whispered, "I missed you."

For a moment, I wondered when was the last time I had seen her.

My throat was parched, and my voice was rough, but I managed to answer, "I missed you too, sweetheart."

I managed to turn my head to see Elisen sitting in a chair, tears of happiness silently rolling down her cheeks. Behind her were my father, Esme, Garry, Odilia, Kelly, Theo, and a few pack members. Why was Elisen crying? Why was everyone here? I didn't understand.

I whispered, "What's going on?"

Elisen crashed into my chest, crying. She sobbed, "You were dead!"

I looked around the room to see my father nod. My heart leaped into my mouth at her words. How could that be? To think of the pain that she had to endure. It must have been unbearable.

I pushed with my arms, and pain shot through my body, but I got into a sitting position. I knew the pain would soon be gone, and I'd be healed. I was thankful for my wolf's healing powers. If I had been dead, then it was a miracle that I could move so fast.

I grabbed Elisen's arm with my left hand and pulled on her so she got closer. I lifted her chin so she would look at me. Her green eyes were filled with sorrow. Seeing her like that tore me apart, and my wolf was getting agitated. All I wanted was to stop this flow of tears. I only wanted to see her smile. I gently wiped the tears off her face, whispering, "I'm here now."

The touch of her lips as I landed a soft kiss created sparkles inside me, and my wolf purred in satisfaction.

My father put a firm hand on my shoulder, a single tear in the corner of his eye. "I'm so glad you're back, my son."

I had never seen my father so emotional, and a knot formed in my stomach to think that all those I loved had been sad by my death.

A question suddenly came to mind, "If I were dead, how is it that I'm alive?"

Kelly stepped forward, and Elisen stepped aside so my friend could embrace me. Her hug was warm and soothing.

"I'm so glad you're back!" she whispered before returning to Theo's side. Then she added, "When you died, Theo and I got your body back here. Elisen ran to her people's realm and got your soul back."

I looked at them, stunned. A faint memory came to my mind: *I was walking, lost, in a crowd of souls, mist as far as the eye could see. And the sudden feeling that my mate was calling me, so clear and precise, amidst it all.*

Elisen continued, "I stole a relic from my people to bring your soul back here. I used an ancient, forbidden song to get your soul back into your body. I'll probably be an outcast forever."

I could hear the pain in her voice. She had sacrificed so much for me! I will be forever grateful to her.

I whispered to her, "I'm in your debt."

She shook her head. "How could you say that? You would have done the same for me!"

I smiled. "True. Still, thank you."

At this moment, all I wanted was to be alone with Elisen. But a small hand squeezed my hand. I looked at my daughter.

"You said you wouldn't leave me alone. I was scared! I thought the man in the wall got you. He said his servant did."

I raised her onto the bed in my arms.

"You say his servant got me?"

The little girl nodded. I kissed the top of her head, squeezing her into my arms.

"I'm sorry, sweetheart. I didn't mean to. But I swear I'll be more careful next time."

The child cuddled in my arms.

I looked at my father with a serious face. "Then the necromancer is the servant on this 'man in the wall.'"

My father clenched his fists. "It seems so."

I took a deep breath. This was a lot to take in at once. I looked around and realized it must have been nighttime as the moon was high in the sky.

"What's everyone doing awake at this time of the night? Don't tell me you were worried about me and stayed up?"

My father shook his head. "I'm afraid a lot has happened while you were gone, my son. It's daytime."

I listened as he explained about the eternal night that had fallen upon us and how Serena had been gone for a while to investigate the cause of it.

My thoughts scrambled as I tried to make sense of everything happening. This was bad, and the fact that Serena wasn't back got me worried. She was a great spell caster, but she was alone.

"The man in the wall wants the sun never to return," explained Molly.

"Let's hope Serena can find the man in the wall, then," I told the child.

An uneasy feeling crept up on me. I added to Elisen through our bond, *"Considering the necromancer is powerful, I can't even imagine how powerful is the man in the wall. Let's hope Serena doesn't try to confront him alone."*

I could feel her agreement through our bond.

"We're still looking for Gregory," added Kelly.

"Gregory?" I asked.

Kelly nodded, and Elisen continued, "I saw him in the forest while searching for your soul. I didn't have time to check on him. He looked disoriented, and I figured he'd return to the pack, but he hasn't."

I could sense how guilty she felt through our bond.

"Don't feel guilty; it's not your fault," I told her gently.

Kelly nodded. "Right. And you had to get Matthew's soul before he went to the afterlife."

I chuckled. "That's kind of important."

She relaxed at our words, nodding. "Thanks, guys. You're right."

We talked for a while, catching up on everything, and everyone was relieved that I was alive. I was just happy to enjoy time with the ones I loved.

Eventually, my father spoke in a serious voice, "More and more people are disappearing. We've had a few zombie attacks in the pack as well. We'll need to fight this necromancer, and soon."

I clenched my jaw when I remembered the ambush we had been caught in. This necromancer was a thorn in my side. The next time we fought him, I needed to be careful not to die. I couldn't wait to be fully healed to end this threat.

"We have prepared spell casters to come with you," Esme said.

My father was about to say something when the window broke into pieces. Instinctively, I grabbed Molly and Elisen in my arms, shielding them from the shards. My wolf growled violently, but my father was there. He was the Alpha; I needed to wait for his orders.

Two women and a man erupted in the room. They had the same purplish skin as Elisen. Judging from the shock on her face, I'd say that she knew them.

My father took a step forward and growled, "What is the meaning of this? How dare you break into my house!"

The older one with white hair seemed to be in charge. She answered, "We came here to get this thief."

My wolf went wild when she pointed to Elisen. She was dreaming if she thought I would hand her away. I would give my life to protect her. Fighting to keep my wolf in check, I looked at my father.

"Elisen is my son's mate. She is part of our pack, and we will protect her accordingly." He gritted through his teeth, his wolf growling violently in his chest.

I relaxed at his words. My father and Garry blocked the path of the intruders. I wanted to join them too, but my father gestured for me to stay where I was, with Molly and Elisen. I had only been revived and wasn't sure how fully healed I was. My father and Garry looked daringly at the nymphs that had broken into the room.

"Elisen stole something very dear to us," the older woman said.

Elisen got up from the bed, grabbed a weird-looking relic on the desk, and brought it to her. "Here, Queen Delijiah. I don't need it anymore."

The queen firmly grabbed her wrist. I jumped from the bed, leaving Molly alone with Odilia and Esme. I grabbed the queen's wrist, slowly saying, "You better let go of her. Now."

My father spoke with authority, "You have your relic. Now let go of the girl and leave."

The queen spat angrily, "I will deal with this thief however I see fit!"

The woman to the queen's right whispered to Elisen, smiling, "That's him."

Elisen answered her, "Yes, Elysia. It's him, my soulmate."

The man didn't say anything. He only stared.

The queen shouted angrily, "None sense! Soul nymphs can't love."

Elisen spat at her, "You're lying! I love him!"

My heart beat vigorously at those words. I ripped the queen's hand from Elisen's wrist and protected her in my arms.

Elisen continued accusing, "You've been lying to everyone! About a lot of things!"

The queen looked offended. "How dare you? Would people believe the words of a tainted thief like yourself? Or those of the pure queen serving them for years?"

Elisen pointed to the two that accompanied the queen, "They can see with their eyes, can't they?"

Elysia smiled. "I can certainly see how much you two love each other."

The man observed, staying silent.

Elisen spoke again, "She lied about many things. Carleon, did you know she had a room full of treasures in her palace?"

The man turned to look at the queen, then back at Elisen. She continued, "I saw all the relics and richness she's hiding when I fetched the soul's vessel."

"You always said we didn't need riches and were a pure race. You said that material belongings hinder the soul. Where do these treasures come from?" asked Carelon to the queen.

"We should be sharing those with everyone! Or exhibiting them in a museum!" exclaimed Elysia.

Delijiah was losing her cool. "She's inventing things! All lies!"

Elisen taunted her, "Lies. Like when you said we couldn't reproduce?"

Delijiah's eyes opened wide. "See? She's lost her mind! That's what happens when we lose the purity of our race to such tainted bastards."

Elisen asked, "If it's a lie, how can you explain this child?"

She pointed to Molly, who was trying to hide in Odilia's arms. I gestured to her, opening my arms. "Come, sweetheart. Don't worry. Daddy will protect you."

The little girl nodded and ran into my arms.

Elysia's eyes widened as she asked, "Is she…?"

Elisen shook her head. "She's our adoptive daughter. But her mother was a soul nymph."

"How can you tell?" yelled the queen. "She doesn't even have our skin tone."

"That's because her father wasn't a soul nymph!" exclaimed Elisen before adding, "She knows our songs! The ones to guide the souls to the afterlife. And she sees the souls flow."

"Lies!" exclaimed the queen.

Carleon stared intensely at Molly, mouth agape. He reached the girl's level, whispering, "Theresa."

Molly squeezed my leg, scared, answering, "That was my mommy's name."

Carelon stared at the girl with tenderness in his eyes. He got back up, pointing at the queen. "You ARE lying to us!"

He turned to us, explaining, "Theresa was one of my good friends. She disappeared a few years ago, and I never heard back from her. But I see her in this child: her eyes, nose, and lips. There can be no mistake."

Elysia spoke in amazement, "Maybe we could have male soul nymphs again if we reproduced? That would be amazing!"

Delijiah shouted, "Are you all going crazy? We've almost achieved pure perfection! A race with only females, no reproduction, and no feelings. Assessing our duties with precision, a race purer than all others."

Carleon exclaimed, "Are you saying males are impure?"

The queen only stared at him in disdain.

Elisen exclaimed, "Males are not tainted! They are loving and protecting. They are wonderful and complete us in ways you can't even understand!"

"Enough!" yelled the queen.

"Indeed enough," said Carleon threateningly to the queen.

She looked at him in surprise, then turned to Elysia, who also pointed her weapons at her.

"Well," snickered Delijiah. "It seems I'll need to make you disappear too. Starting with HER!" she yelled the last word and lunged to grab Molly.

I shielded the child in my arms as Elisen screamed, "Don't touch my daughter!"

My father turned into his wolf, joined by Garry. I returned Molly back with Odilia while Esme cast a protective bubble around them. Elisen, Carleon, and Elysia jumped on the queen. My father howled for the pack to join us. I let my wolf take control as I joined the fight, pulled by my Alpha's command.

The queen offered a bigger resistance than anticipated. Other wolves from the pack joined our fight. I slashed at her while others bit her. We kept attacking from all sides. Soon, Delijiah was overrun. Carleon's sword gave the final blow. The queen's body fell to the floor, blood pooling around it.

A small cry caught my attention as I savored the scent of blood and victory. It was Molly. The fight scared her, and she was crying. My paternal instinct took over, and I transformed into my human form to comfort her. Elisen also came and hugged us. Together as a family, Molly calmed herself.

Elysia searched the dead queen's body as people from my pack returned to their human forms. She soon retrieved a glowing jewel from her chest.

She handed it to Elisen. "Here, it should be yours."

Elisen stared at the gem. "I… I can't take this."

"What is it?" I asked.

Elysia answered, "It's the queen's sacred gem. The one who possesses it becomes the next queen. When the coronation ceremony is done, it embeds itself into the queen's body."

Elisen looked at her friend. "My place is here. With Matthew and Molly and the pack. You should take it."

"Are you sure?" asked Elysia.

Elisen nodded. "You will make an amazing queen!"

Carleon put a hand on his heart. "It will be an honor to serve you!"

Elysia nodded. "Okay, but promise me you'll visit."

"Of course!" exclaimed Elisen. "I'll show Molly the domain where her mother was born."

Elysia and Carleon apologized to the Alpha for breaking into the pack's house. They stayed for a while, getting to know the pack and our culture. Elisen talked to Molly about her mother's heritage, and Carleon was happy to talk about Theresa to Molly.

It was heartwarming, and I was happy to learn more about my mate's race. But Elysia and Carleon promised to visit once in a while to create the first treaty between the soul nymphs and the werewolves. I only wish I could see their realm.

Eventually, Elysia and Carleon gave their farewell. With the death of the queen and everything she's been hiding, they had a lot of work waiting for them in their domain.

My father exclaimed, "Let's take the rest of the day to repair the damage to the house and rest. We'll deal with the necromancer tomorrow."

Elisen and I spent the afternoon playing in the yard with Molly. Esme had sent a few fairies with us, giving a colorful display of light as my daughter ran around the yard. It was hard to believe it was midday. I had no problems seeing in the dark, thanks to my enhanced lycanthrope sight, but Elisen and Molly needed the fairies' light.

I was grateful for the Alpha blood that ran through my veins. Thanks to my regenerating powers, I didn't feel any after-effects of dying. I watched in awe how the two ladies of my life played together. It was beautiful to see Molly laughing heartily as Elisen tickled her. She made a wonderful mother.

Thinking I had died was an unsettling thought. I didn't know what I would have done if I had been in Elisen's place. Just thinking about it made my wolf restless. I was lost, trying to find a way to keep them safe. One thing was for sure: I needed to seal the bond with Elisen. I never wanted to be separated from my mate or my daughter again.

Hours passed by. Elisen and I sat together in our room as Molly slept in hers.

"We're finally alone," I purred on her skin as I kissed her neck.

She sighed in delight, cuddling closer to me.

"I missed you so much," she confessed. "I can't even describe the sadness that I felt."

A surge of despair filled me as her feelings passed through our bonds, giving me an idea of how she felt. I lowered my gaze as my chest tightened. I felt guilty for the pain she had to endure because of me.

"I'm sorry," I whispered. "I wish I could change what happened."

She put her hand on my chest. "It wasn't your fault. I just…" Her green eyes laid on mine, an unspoken promise shining into them. "I never want to be separated from you again."

A growl of need escaped my chest. I grabbed her hand, kissing her knuckles softly, my wolf yearning for her.

"Then, will you allow me to mark you?"

"Mark me?"

I nodded. "Yes. Seal our bond, so our souls intertwine, never to be separated again."

"Does this mean we'd spend the afterlife together? Is this even possible?"

Passion filled me as I spoke, "There's no doubt in my mind that it is."

And it was true. I truly believed the Moon Goddess would grant us eternity together. Elisen's eyes glimmered as she answered, "Let's do it. I want to love you forever."

As my wild instincts took hold of me, Elisen's sweet scent of lilac started driving me crazy, nearly making me lose whatever hold I still had over my body. My wolf kept repeating one word over and over, "Mine." He was trying to take control, and I could already feel my sense heighten.

I kissed Elisen's luscious lips as I explained, "To seal our bond, I need to mark you. With my wolf's teeth, I will bite you. It will create a mark forever saying that you are mine."

Elisen quivered in my arms, "Bite me?"

I nodded. "I will make sure it doesn't hurt."

She nodded as she stared into my eyes. I could read an understanding and trust only lovers share in her gaze. She knew I wouldn't hurt her and would keep my promise.

Her body already felt hot as her naughty hands roamed my body. My wolf was gnawing for me to take her as the smell of her arousal grew stronger.

I grunted when she caught my erection. Speaking was getting harder. "Every wolf will know you're my mate… And… Fuck!" I groaned as she stroked me harder.

My wolf finally took control as I devoured her lips, my tongue dancing with hers. It took all my efforts not to rip off her clothes. She was deliciously enticing, and I was getting intoxicated by her. I kissed my way down her legs, kissing her inner thighs while caressing her body. I loved the shivers that appeared when I grazed every inch of her soft skin. I licked her juices as she groaned in reward. I grabbed her hip as she began to thrust, holding her in place so I could continue to ravish her, the melodious sound of her voice leaving me even more eager to take her.

Her clit was swollen and needed my attention. I circled on it, letting her sweet moans guide me. I kept licking and circling her clit until she finally screamed as she peaked, her legs shaking. She grabbed the sheets as she arched her back, her head tilted upward, aspiring for more. This was truly the most beautiful sight I could ever lay my eyes on.

My cock was rock hard, and I needed her more than ever. I made my way up, nibbling and biting gently at her nipples, earning a few more moans. The tip of my cock was just touching her entrance, a sweet temptation. Breathless, she whispered between kisses, "I love you so much, Matthew."

My wolf purred with love as I whispered, "I will forever love you from the bottom of my heart."

I penetrated her as my tongue swirled with hers, her hard nipples brushing against me as she arched her back in pleasure, moaning in my mouth. Waves of pleasure washed over me instantly. She was so perfect, and my wolf took pride in the fact that we were the ones to make her writhe like that. I thrust into her hard, adjusting to her cries. Drowning in pleasure, I soon lost whatever hold I had on my instincts. My canines grew, and my wolf growled with excitement. I looked at her once more. Her lustful eyes met mine for a moment. She noticed my teeth and cried as I pushed deeper into her, "Yes!" It was both a cry of pleasure and acquiescence.

Her fingers dug into my back as I sank my teeth where the neck met the shoulder, just deep enough that it pierced the skin. In an instant, I felt connected with her more than ever, feeling her love, thoughts, and pleasure from inside and out.

She screamed, "Oh, fuck, that's good!"

Wrapped in this blissful moment, I kept thrusting into her as our souls weaved together perfectly. Her climax came first, and I almost came immediately as I felt it through our bond before feeling her walls pulse around me. I kept thrusting slower as I removed my teeth from her neck, my tongue lingering on the spot where I had bitten her to let the wound heal.

Drunk from her pleasure and mine, I kept thrusting, feeling her pleasure heighten again. I kept pushing, deep and strong, hard as rock, until she climaxed again. I groaned her name as I came hard when her second climax hit me. I kept thrusting, wrapped in her pleasure and mine, an indescribable feeling of bliss. I finally slowed my thrust, laying by her side but keeping her close.

Elisen looked at me with her emerald eyes, staring at my soul. In this moment, holding my mate in my arms, I had everything I could ever need. My breath was hot on her neck as I whispered, "I will give my life to protect you. I will kill whoever harms you."

She shook her head, her fingers resting on my chest while my wolf purred with love. "I don't want you to die for me, Matt. I want you by my side."

She brushed her nails on my chest, making goosebumps appear on their trail. Her lips were soft when she kissed me, my heart fluttering as I loved her so much. I grabbed her hips and rested my forehead with hers. "All right. Then I promise you. I will always stay by your side."

She smiled in satisfaction. I could feel Elisen relax as she listened to my wolf's purr. I heard her whisper in my mind, "This, right now, is paradise."

Her smile widened as I whispered back through our bond, "Then prepare to enjoy paradise every day, love."

I held her close to me as we fell asleep together.

Chapter 16 (Matthew)

Erebus

Sweet kisses tingled on my neck, and my heart beat strongly.

"Hm… Good morning," I whispered with a hoarse voice. I opened my eyes to see my beautiful Elisen smiling at me.

"Sorry to wake you up," her melodious voice resonated through my soul. "Our daughter has been knocking at our door."

A slight tap came at the door as she spoke those words, and I chuckled. I must have been exhausted not to hear it earlier. But thanks to my Alpha blood, and a full night of rest, I was now feeling completely healed and ready to put an end to the necromancer.

"Come in, sweetheart," I said to Molly.

The little girl opened the door and ran into our bed to hug us. I smiled at the thought that my mornings would be filled with warm hugs. If someone had told me I'd be a father at twenty-six years old, I would have told them they were crazy. Especially since I had been born on a sacred night, destined to be sacrificed. My life had significantly changed in a short time, but I couldn't be happier.

My father was talking with Esme when we got down. Molly ran into his arms. He turned to us. "Ah, there you are! The team is assembled and waiting outside."

Esme added, "A team of spell casters is also waiting."

Molly pouted her lips. "Do you really need to go?"

I caressed her cheek. "Yes. We need to deal with the bad guys. But we'll be back, I promise."

The little girl crossed her arms. "That's what you said last time."

I sighed. She was right. "I know," I whispered. "But this time, I have a whole team fighting with me. And I'll be more careful."

Molly pursed her lips, looking at me with wide eyes. "Do you promise?"

I nodded to her, and her lip curled up slightly. Elisen added, "I'll look after him. We'll both be back."

Molly grinned, showing her pearly whites.

Odilia entered the pack's house with Garry. She looked happy while holding his hand, and I was glad that she had found her mate, especially after what had happened to her. My father stepped toward them.

"Odilia. Thank you for coming!"

She nodded. "It's my pleasure, my Alpha."

My father nodded, happy. He let Molly on the floor, caressing the girl's hair.

"I leave Molly with you while my son goes to the battle."

"Really?" asked the little girl, excitement sparkling in her eyes.

"Of course!" exclaimed Odilia, "it's a pleasure!"

I knew how much Molly loved Odilia and Garry. She even called them her aunt and uncle. I would ensure our house would be close to theirs once we moved the pack to a new place. This way, Molly could visit her aunt and uncle as much as she wanted.

I hugged my daughter one last time and left the pack house with a light heart, knowing she would be well cared for.

At least thirty men and women were waiting for me outside. I could feel the wolves in at least two-thirds of the group. As for the others, they didn't have a wolf but had magical power. They were the spell casters. I was impressed and nervous. It was my first time directing such a big group. To think my father had to lead the whole pack all the time. I would need to ask him for advice before taking the pack's lead. Hopefully, I still have a few years to learn.

Elisen grabbed my hand, and all my stress disappeared. She whispered through our bond, *"Don't worry. You'll make an amazing leader."*

I squeezed her hand lovingly.

My shoulders felt heavy from the gaze of all those fighters. All eyes were riveted on me. I raised my head high, trying to be the Alpha they wanted me to be. I took a deep breath, thinking of something to say to them.

I spoke loudly as I slowly paced, "My friends, tonight we fight for all our lost friends and loved ones. We will no longer be afraid of losing our families. We will kill the necromancer. Tonight we get our freedom back!"

It wasn't much of a speech, but I smiled proudly when they cheered. Behind me, Elisen was smiling gently.

We started walking toward the woods. Just as we ventured into the woods, we ran into a group of fifty humans and werewolves from another pack who were hunting down the necromancer. Joining our forces, we were even stronger.

It was still dark, as the sun hadn't been up for days. Adrenaline ran through my veins as we walked. I had to be careful not to get killed this time. I had to protect my mate, and we needed to go back home to our daughter. I was looking forward to being done dealing with the necromancer so that I could live happily with Elisen and Molly.

"It will be wonderful," Elisen spoke through my mind.

Serena's POV

We stayed silent as voices echoed on the walls. There were two female voices and one deep male voice. As we got closer, we began to understand the words they were saying.

"You can't keep me here forever!" shouted the first female.

"Watch me!" growled the male.

"It's only for a while," added the other female.

"Traitors!" shouted the first female.

"Shut up, or I'll kill you right now!" barked the male.

We soon arrived at a large and dark cave. The only light came from a fire at the back of the room. Near it was a big metallic cage; I saw a woman inside it. Her long, elegant beige dress was torn and dirty. Her skin was white, and her brown hair came to her hips. She wore golden bracelets. Although she was dirty, her grace shone through. I gasped when I recognized her from the destroyed pictures in the shrine. This was Hemera, Goddess of the Day. Jasper put his hand on my mouth, reminding me we needed to stay silent.

I heard in my mind, *"Tell me through our bond like this."*

Right, I hadn't thought about that.

I pushed to his mind, *"This is Hemera! The Goddess of the Day."*

He asked, *"Do you know who they are?"*

A woman paced back and forth nervously at the center of the room. Her hair was black as night, and her icy blue eyes shone in the darkness. She wore a lace-up bustier revealing her ample breasts, with an asymmetrical black skirt and leather boots. A shimmer-through cape flowed behind her as she walked. Beside the fire stood a tall man wearing only black pants. His chest was even more muscular than Jasper's. He held two long swords, one in each hand. His skin was black as charcoal. His eyes were red, and his hair was black. Two black feathered wings came out of his back. A dark and stormy aura seemed to follow him as he moved. Seeing him made the hairs on the back of my neck stand up.

Jasper squeezed my hand lovingly, reminding me he would protect me.

"This must be Erebus, the demon of darkness," I pushed through his mind before adding, *"And she must be Nyx, the Goddess of the night."*

Jasper studied them closely before asking through our bond.

"What's a Goddess doing with a demon?"

"Didn't you learn about them in history?"

I could feel his shame through our bond as he answered, *"As a guard at the vampires' palace, I was allowed to skip classes to train. I didn't like school very much."*

"Don't be embarrassed. Nyx is Erebus's wife. Hemera is their daughter."

I could feel his surprise at this statement.

"I guess we need to free Hemera, then," he pushed through my mind.

Although, I still felt like I should get the rest of the pack.

Jasper asked through my mind, *"This is important to you, right?"*

I nodded. *"Yes, my pack is my family. We always act together."*

He nodded back. *"Right, then let's back off silently and get them."*

"Are you coming with me?"

He grinned. *"Of course! I'm your mate! I would never let you go alone!"*

I smiled and started to turn around, silently returning to the tunnel we came in from.

Erebus growled with rage.

"How dare she imprison my son, Eurynomos! That bitch is going to pay!"

That's when I realized he was talking about the Moon Goddess.

The walls shook from his anger. Loose rocks fell from the ceiling. I shrieked when Jasper pushed me just in time to avoid getting hit by one.

My heart stopped beating when they all turned toward us. So much for being silent. The demon narrowed his eyes at me and spoke with hatred, "You… You're one of the goddess's wards."

Jasper's eyes landed on me. *"Are you?"*

Our pack's duty was to keep Eurynomos sealed for the Moon Goddess.

I pushed back in his mind, *"Sort of...."*

I didn't have time to explain further as the demon jumped on me, dust and debris flying under the breath of his wings. I flicked my wrist, sending a bolt of lightning his way, but he avoided it easily. His body crashed into mine, pinning me to the ground. The pain seared through my head as I hit the floor. My vision blurred, and I could only see a flash of light for a moment. I could feel Erebus's weight on me, suffocating me. I regained sight just in time to see his fist coming straight at me. Pinned like that, I couldn't cast a spell. Close combat was not my forte. Luckily, a strong hand stopped Erebus's hand just before my face. Erebus took a step back, staring at him. Jasper's eyes were red, his fangs were grown, and his nails were sharp. He growled angrily, the sound filling the chamber.

"Don't you touch my mate!" Jasper spat at the demon before jumping on him.

The two of them started fighting. A storm raged inside Jasper's head, his strength now matching the demon's power. They swirled as they fought in the air, their blood mixing, black feathers falling to the ground. I watched their display of force in awe when I realized that Nyx was preparing to interfere.

I launched a lightning bolt just in time to deflect the spell she was casting at Jasper, bouncing it off the wall before it died. The Goddess of the night hissed at me.

"Annoying witch! Don't you dare interfere with our plans."

"And what is it that you're planning?"

"Eternal night."

I scoffed, "And how will you do so?"

The goddess snickered. "We will kill our daughter."

I shouted, surprised, "What? Would you kill your own child? And for what?"

"Eurynomos has been sealed for years now. All because of that Moon Goddess bitch."

I rolled my eyes.

"Eternal night doesn't seem like a great way to get back at the Moon Goddess."

She sneered at me.

"Don't you see? We'll take revenge on Eurynomos's keepers: you and your vile pack. You will learn the price for agreeing to become her wards. We will take revenge on the living. All the things the Moon Goddess cherishes. When everything is dying, she will have no choice but to show herself. That's when we will strike."

My eyes widened as I realized the extent of their plan: she planned to make everything die slowly. Plants would surely die first from the lack of light. Soon plant-feeding creatures would follow; before the carnivores perished. The world would become a barren darkness, empty of living beings. An eternal nightmare filled with silence. Only gods and demons would survive.

"What good would such an empty world be to you?"

The goddess rolled her eyes.

"Such a stupid girl! The night is my domain, and darkness is my husband's. I don't care about living beings. They are only an annoyance in my existence."

I realized now how dangerous these two were. It was beyond anything I could have imagined. My hands were shaking, but I sent a fireball at the goddess. She quickly countered it with a flow of ice.

She yelled at me, "Think you can take on a goddess? Impudent fool!"

She launched a wave of magic toward me, but I cast a shield before me. Magic was my element. I felt confident. The sound of Jasper fighting with Erebus filled the room as dust and rocks fell. I launched magic bolts and ribbons at Nyx, but she kept countering them. She was fast. Doubt started to creep into my mind. Was I strong enough to fight a goddess?

Jasper's voice echoed in my mind, *"I believe in you, love."*

My heart raced at those words. I sent a series of lightning bolts at the goddess. One scorched her cheek, leaving a burned trail across her perfect white cheek. Nyx screamed with rage and redoubled her efforts against me. Her attacks were getting stronger, making me recoil as they hit me. It was getting evident that I couldn't win against her.

It occurred to me that I should try to free Hemera. Surely it would help to have a goddess on our side.

I tried to approach the cage, but Nyx didn't let me. I sent a bolt of lightning toward the wall behind Nyx. The lightning bolt bounced back on the wall and landed on the cage's door.

Nyx laughed. "Can't even aim at me to save her life! Stupid mortal."

This was precisely what I was hoping for. I didn't want her to think I was trying to break Hemera free. I wanted her to believe I was still aiming at her.

Hemera glanced at me. She understood what I was doing and stepped back from the door. One bolt wasn't enough, but I hoped several would do the trick. I kept shooting my magic toward Nyx, purposely missing my mark, so it bounced back onto the cage's door. Nyx was full of confidence. She honestly thought I was missing all my hits and that she would easily win this battle. She kept attacking me, but I dodged her attacks. Little did she know that the cage's door was almost broken. I glanced for a moment at Jasper, still fighting Erebus. He was wounded, but he was still standing strong. I felt pleased to have such a strong mate, but I knew he couldn't stand up to a demon alone.

I whispered through our bond, *"Hang on, my love. Help is coming."*

Just as I felt Jasper's incomprehension through our bond, the cage door broke open.

Nyx's eyes widened as Hemera came out of the cage, and Erebus cursed.

"Now's the time to get back to the Underworld," the Goddess of the Day declared sternly.

Nyx shouted, "No!"

Erebus turned his attention away from Jasper and faced Hemera. "We are so close now. There's no way we're going to let you ruin it. Now it's your turn to die, dear *daughter*."

Erebus and Nyx launched themselves at Hemera. I created the strongest shield I could in front of her, and Jasper threw himself at Erebus. Hemera's magic was as strong as the sun. Shedding light in the darkness, she was cutting through Nyx's magic. Erebus was trying to get at her, but she would push him back with her palm as if it were merely a fly. It was clear she was stronger than the demon and the evil goddess.

I sent a fireball toward Nyx, and Jasper tried to sink his fangs into Erebus's neck. This fight had lasted long enough; it was time to end this. But Hemera turned toward us, stopping us, smiling, her face bright as day.

"You have done more than enough. I can handle it from here."

She grabbed Nyx and Erebus with a magical cord, trapping them together.

We stepped back and watched Hemera handle her parents. Jasper set his arms around me, surrounding me with his manly scent that I loved so much. I settled against his body as I watched in awe how Hemera easily took care of the evil goddess and the demon.

She explained, "This is the magical lasso that was given to me by Zeus. Nyx and Erebus have no power against it. It is how I can force them back to the Underworld, bringing the day back."

I watched how Nyx and Erebus fought against the lasso. However hard they fought, they couldn't get away. It only got tighter the harder they fought. Nyx tried to send magic toward us, but Hemera stopped it easily.

"Hush now. You've done way more than enough for today," Hemera whispered to her parents.

They both lashed out at her words, shouting insults at her.

Chapter 17 (Elisen)

Bad omen

We didn't get very far. I could hear the low grunt of the zombies in the dead of night. It sounded unnatural, and nature listened silently to their footsteps. Soon, a swarm of undead came into view. They stretched as far as the eye could see, far into the woods, way past their lair. What were they doing this far? Were they preparing an attack? My heart froze: we couldn't let them get to the pack and to Molly. This needed to end here!

Most zombies wore leather armor and brandished a thick piece of metal as a sword, while others had a stick. Some of them had lost the skin on their skulls, the cranial sutures giving them a patched appearance. Others had flesh peeling off their faces. The smell of rotten flesh was fetid, and I swallowed back the bile in my mouth. This was an atrocious sight, truly unholy, and it was time we put an end to this.

Panic rose in me when Matthew gestured to go forward.

"Don't!" I screamed.

Our fighters stared at me as I explained, "The other day, Matthew was killed by a strong spell. We're all at risk!"

Whispers rose from our warriors. Matthew wrapped his arms around me. "You're right."

I stared at his blue eyes. "I wouldn't want you to die again."

He caressed my cheek lovingly, saying, "I wouldn't want anything happening to you."

"We can help!" a woman shouted through our fighters. People got out of their way, and the group of spell casters came forward.

"We can cast a shell spell around everyone. It will greatly lessen the effects of enemy spells and prevent you from dying from a magical source."

I relaxed at those words.

I answered, "Great, this is exactly what we need!"

The spell caster looked at everyone.

"Get together in groups of ten. We will cast a spell on you. But the effect will only last fifteen minutes."

A knot formed in my stomach at this last statement. But Matthew's hand landed on my shoulder, reassuring me. He spoke strongly and confidently, "Then we will kill them all in under fifteen minutes."

People nodded and cheered at his words. I loved how good of a leader he was. People were happy to follow him and trusted him.

"Thanks, my love," answered a cocky voice in my head.

I smirked at Matthew. He only showed me this side of his personality, and I loved it. I hugged him while the spell casters protected us, keeping an eye on the zombies, who, luckily, hadn't seen us yet.

As soon as they were done casting, we rushed through the enemies. We only had fifteen minutes before the spell wore out; we couldn't afford to lose precious time.

Matthew changed into his wolf. He bit the zombies while I slashed through the enemies with my swords. We stayed together while our fighters kept fighting the zombies, beheading them. Matthew's and my goal was the necromancer. Adrenaline pumped through my veins, and my heart raced as we moved forward in the swarm of zombies. A sense of calm filled me as we decimated the enemy's army. One by one, the bodies piled on the floor. With Matthew by my side, I felt invincible.

Slowly, Matthew and I were making our way forward, further than the group. It seemed there was no end to the zombies. Every time we killed one, another appeared.

Suddenly, I saw a crown appear over the crowd. There he was, only a little further. I couldn't see him yet, but I knew it was the necromancer. Matthew's wolf growled threateningly.

Just as we were about to move closer to him, three ghostly women appeared out of thin air. Their hair floated through the air as if blown by an invisible wind. Their eyes were white without pupils. They all wore majestic white dresses that floated around them as they flew. I knew what they were. My blood ran cold. One word resonated through my head as Matthew spoke through our bond, *"Banshees."*

The fact they were here wasn't a good omen. I had heard that when several banshees appear at once, it indicates the death of someone great or holy. Fear crept into my mind, and I started to cry, a pain radiating through my chest. Matthew turned to his human form and pulled me into his arms as the banshees screamed together. It was a deafening high pitch sound, and everyone stopped momentarily, shivering in fright at the banshees' cry. A high-pitched noise filled my ears for a split second, even after the banshees had stopped screaming. I wondered if I had gone deaf, hearing only silence, but to my relief, the sounds returned after a few seconds. The banshees disappeared as quickly as they had appeared, leaving us wondering whose death they were announcing.

As if reading my mind, Matthew said confidently, "I'm not dying today, and you're not either."

I pulled myself together, took a deep breath, and nodded. "Right."

He stole a kiss on my lips, igniting my heart, before pushing further.

As we got closer to the necromancer, I got the eerie feeling that I had seen him before. I could see curly, light brown hair coming from under the crown. His eyes looked like they were staring at the void but were the same blue I had seen before. Just as I was about to say it, Matthew shouted incredulously, "Gregory?"

He had been missing, and people had been searching all over for him. The necromancer stared at us, cold as ice. His eyes narrowed as he hissed in a very low voice, "How the fuck are you still alive? I got rid of you."

I watched, baffled, as Matthew shook his head. "What the fuck are you talking about, Gregory?"

The necromancer answered, "I don't know whom you're talking about. My name is DeMörder."

"Stop your bullshit, Gregory!" shouted Matthew.

The necromancer grabbed his head in pain with his hands. His eyes softened, and he spoke with a soft, innocent voice, "It wasn't me, Matthew. I swear it wasn't me. I just…"

His voice suddenly darkened, "Of course, it was me! Never will I be this weak fool that you saw."

I watched it all, unable to say a word. Matthew shouted, "Come on, Gregory. I've always been there for you."

Gregory crawled to the floor, crying and removing the crown. "Everyone kept laughing at me. I was so useless. All I wanted to do was to help…."

Matthew reached out his hand to him. "Come on, Gregory. Let's go back to the pack together. Stop this madness."

Gregory stopped talking at once and straightened up. His face was stern and angry, his eyes glowing darkly. He shouted in a deep voice, "Enough! This is over. You will now face my wrath!"

I still couldn't get over the fact that Gregory and DeMörder were the same person, but I didn't have time to process the idea properly. DeMörder was walking toward us. He was furious. A dark magic aura surrounded him, and I was downright scared. Matthew's wolf growled menacingly as DeMörder walked toward me. He shielded me with his body, but I didn't want him to die.

Matthew gritted the words through his teeth, "I can't believe it was you all along. To think I trusted you."

DeMörder cracked his neck, smiling wickedly. "What a fool you were."

I took a fighting stance as Matthew and DeMörder also prepared for battle.

Matthew's POV

All around us, our fighters were still battling the zombies. The sound of clashing swords, spurting blood, and falling corpses filled the night. None of this mattered at the moment, as a deafening silence filled my ears. I was stunned. Never in my life had I felt so betrayed. I had protected him when he was mocked. Had I missed something? Was there a sign I hadn't seen? Now I understood how he knew where to find the zombies. And how he was there when we tried to get the relic. He was always there and always looked so innocent.

"I don't think he's right in his mind," whispered Elisen.

I watched how DeMörder seemed to be conversing on his own, switching from Gregory to the dark necromancer. It was as if two completely different entities lived inside the same person.

"He may have a multiple personality disorder, but that doesn't excuse the atrocities he committed," I replied, hatred for this execrable being transpiring in my voice.

I had helped Gregory so many times. And here he was, harvesting a dark power, killing people, and raising the dead to fight against us. I clenched my fists, my nails digging into my skin.

Just then, a shriek echoed in the night.

"Let go of me!"

My heart froze as I knew that voice without even looking. My fear was confirmed when I turned my head to see Molly being dragged by a man.

DeMörder turned to him with a grin. "Ah, Judah! You're just in time."

I screamed, "Let go of my daughter!"

Molly turned her head toward us. "Mommy! Daddy! Help!"

Elisen and I motioned to get her, but DeMörder shook his head wickedly, pointing to Judah.

"I wouldn't do this if I were you."

We turned to Judah, who was holding a knife to Molly's neck.

DeMörder continued, "You move, she dies."

I clenched my fists. I was desperate to save my daughter, but she would be killed if I tried anything. This was dirty. How could he involve a child in this? All I wanted to do at this moment was to tear this sick bastard apart.

I gritted my teeth. "What do you want with her?"

He cracked his neck. "Me? Nothing. But Erebus has instructed me to kill her."

I cursed as I heard the demon's name.

"No!" shrieked Molly in a high voice while being dragged closer to the necromancer.

"Why?" I raged.

DeMörder continued, "Erebus says she's special. She's a pure soul, born of an ancient line of sacred people."

I frowned a tightening in my chest. "You mean the soul nymphs?"

The necromancer's eyes darkened. "I mean that one of the girl's parents was a half-angel."

My heart raced when I learned of Molly's father's legacy. I knew nothing about half-angels, but it didn't change that Molly was my daughter, and I wouldn't let her be killed.

I spoke to Elisen through our bond, *"As soon as he lets go of Molly, even for a moment, you run and get her. I'll protect you both."*

Elisen wanted to protest, but I didn't let her. My wolf was on the loose, and soon, I wouldn't be able to hold him. I pushed through her mind, *"Do as I say. It's my time to protect you."*

With the Alpha's blood running through my veins, my wolf needed to prove he could protect them. He needed to save his daughter. Elisen nodded, and I was grateful she didn't try to argue.

At this point, Judah was fairly close to the necromancer. He pushed Molly toward DeMörder to get her to step over the two steps that separated her from him. In doing so, he let go of her, and the knife was no longer held against her neck.

I shouted, "Now!"

Elisen ran and grabbed Molly in her arms before DeMörder could reach her. Judah was just a step too far to reach her.

I jumped on Judah, pushing him to the floor. His knife fell to the ground as his head hit the ground. I was straddling on top of him, pinning his hand to the ground to stop him from reaching for his knife.

Beside me, I could hear Elisen struggle with DeMörder.

I pushed through her mind, *"Get to safety with Molly. I'll deal with them."*

She answered, *"I will, as soon as I get away from him."*

Panic rose inside me at those words. Was she okay? Did she need my help? But I couldn't worry about them as I needed to deal with Judah first.

Judah snarled as he pushed with all his strength to be freed from my grasp, but I was stronger than him. Alpha blood ran through my veins. The man had no chance.

Molly screamed again in fear, and Elisen hit DeMörder. Rage filled me. It was Judah who had abducted my daughter from the pack and brought her here. It was him that had put her life at risk. The man would pay.

I snickered at him. "You took away my daughter. You will regret taking what's mine, boy…."

His eyes flashed with incomprehension. I hit his face. He tried retaliating, but I was faster and stronger. I kept hitting him until he was dazed. I grabbed the fallen knife on the floor and stabbed it into his chest.

"No!" screamed DeMörder, letting go of Molly and running to Judah's side.

Elisen grabbed Molly into her arms, and I joined them.

"What have you done?" asked DeMörder. "Judah! Stay with me, Son! You can't leave me!"

The man smiled faintly at the necromancer. He whispered to him, "It was… an honor… to serve you, master."

DeMörder held the man in his arms as he died. When Judah had given his last breath, DeMörder turned to me. "You killed him! He was like a son to me!"

I gritted, "Just as you intended to do to my daughter!"

DeMörder spoke in disdain, "But his life was important. Hers is worthless."

A low menacing growl escaped my chest. My wolf had this primal urge to destroy this traitor. Heat spread through my body as my wolf took hold of my human body. My sense heightened, and I knew right then and there that I was in a blood lust, even if I was in my human form. This wouldn't end before one of us was dead.

Elisen's eyes widened. "Matt, your eyes are glowing golden!"

I looked at her briefly. "You're seeing my wolf's eyes."

She asked, "How is it possible?"

I answered, "Take Molly and get to a safe distance."

I turned my attention to DeMörder. He was casting a spell on me, probably trying to pull off the same trick he had done the other day. I let him finish his spell, knowing what would happen. His look of incomprehension when it didn't work was worth it. My lip curled upward, and I snickered. "Are your old tricks deceiving you?"

He gushed with anger, "What kind of sorcery is this? I am stronger! I have the demon's power! I will assert my revenge!"

I scoffed. "Face it, sorcerer. You're as worthless as you ever were."

DeMörder grunted as he cast spell after spell on me, each time failing. His eyes glimmered with rage when he realized magic wouldn't work.

"Matt!" shrieked Elisen when zombies jumped on her, trying to get to Molly.

DeMörder was smiling wickedly.

"Coward!" I screamed in rage. He instructed his army to destroy Elisen and Molly since he couldn't kill me.

I grabbed a sword on the ground, killing two zombies that were on Elisen while she killed the others. Free again, she looked toward the necromancer, shouting, "He's getting away!"

The zombies were still swarming us, but our fighters held them off.

Elisen grabbed Molly in her arms, shouting through the noise, "We'll be fine! Go!"

I nodded. I wouldn't let that bastard get away once again.

"Careful!" shouted one of our spell casters. "You don't have much time before the spell wears off."

I shrugged his concern off and ran after DeMörder. With my heightened sense, he was easy to follow. My wolf roared at the trail of fear he was leaving behind him.

I caught up easily with him, my wolf giving me energy and making me run faster than I would normally. He was out of breath, leaning against a tree, his skin looking pale when I saw him.

He motioned to run again, but I stopped him. "Give it up and fight me, already."

DeMörder struggled to stay upright. He looked around and spotted a deer nearby. I watched as he channeled a spell toward the animal. A second later, the animal was dead, and DeMörder looked better.

"What did you do to him?" I asked.

The necromancer's smile looked wicked. "Just a small trick I do to rejuvenate myself."

DeMörder charged me with his staff, but I parried his attack with my sword. I was surprised at how strong he was. Considering that I was the next Alpha in line, only the demon's power could make him so strong. We exchanged a couple of blows, the sorcerer's staff glowing with a dark aura each time my sword hit it. That's when I realized he was imbuing it as we fought. Surely, his mana wasn't endless.

I fought harder, pushing with the strength of my wolf, forcing DeMörder to back with every blow. It was only him and I, surrounded by trees in the dead of night. My wolf was getting restless. He wanted the necromancer's blood to be spilled, and I roared angrily as I forced DeMörder to the ground. He was kneeling on the floor, barely pushing back with his staff again. Black veins started to show through his almost translucent skin.

"What's the matter, sorcerer?" I mocked. "What happened to your almighty powers?"

DeMörder breathed heavily, his voice barely audible, "… Need… to… regenerate."

"So soon? How ironic how the dark power consumes you, isn't it?"

He gestured toward me, trying to suck my life force, but I sank my blade into his heart and spat angrily, "No, you don't!"

His eyes widened, and his mouth opened, a gasp of surprise exiting as he exhaled the air from his lungs. His hand fell, and he whispered softly, "All I wanted… was to be accepted."

I looked at the sick man, dark power ravaging his mind and body. A mix of hate and pity filled me at the sight of this man I once called a friend. His blood was pouring to the ground, and my wolf calmed once he realized the fight was over.

"Bonding with a demon is not the right way to make friends," I answered coldly.

Whatever his intentions were, they couldn't excuse his wicked actions. Coldly killing hundreds, kidnapping my daughter, and trying to kill us. He wouldn't have hesitated to kill me if the spell caster's magic had worn off. I didn't feel guilty for putting him out of his misery.

I watched, waiting for the last drop of blood to leave his body. I knew it was over when I saw his chest no longer rise.

A scream resonated through the forest, "Matthew!"

"Elisen!" I screamed back.

I turned around to see my sweet Elisen running toward me, Molly in her arms, along with Kelly, Theo, and a few fighters.

"You're safe!" She lunged into my arms, Molly's arms embracing me as well, and I embraced them, my heart beating strong. Tears of relief ran down their cheeks. I wiped their tears. Elisen put Molly on the ground. I embraced Elisen and brought her mouth to mine, kissing her softly.

Kelly smiled. "We knew it was over when all the zombies fell to the ground, rapidly decaying. We could hear their souls scream, finally free, and see a dark shroud escaping the corpses."

Elisen continued, "Their souls will finally be able to go to the afterlife. The soul's flow will be restored, and life will return to its normal course."

Molly spoke softly, "We need to sing the song."

Elisen nodded. "You're right. We need to sing the song to guide their souls. But don't worry; others will take care of that."

The little girl nodded.

I looked at the eternal darkness surrounding us. I hoped Serena would succeed and that the sun would rise again.

"Let's go home. We need to report to my father."

Elisen nodded. Theo added, "We also need to decide what to do with DeMörder's followers."

I frowned. "I thought the zombies were dead?"

He nodded. "Yes. But he also had living followers."

I wondered, for a moment, who in their right mind would want to join sides with a necromancer?

"Right, like the one I killed, Judah. Did you catch them all?"

"We think so."

I hoped none of them had the chance to escape. I nodded, "Good job. Let's bring them to my father. As Alpha, he'll decide what to do with them."

We all started walking back to the pack. Our fighters were keeping a close eye on the necromancer's followers. A sense of peace filled me at the thought that I'd finally be able to enjoy time with my mate and my daughter.

Chapter 18 (Serena)

Sunflower

Hemera opened a portal to the Underworld. I watched her from the safety of Jasper's arms as she dragged Nyx and Erebus back where they belonged.

As she did, the light made its way through the cave. We stepped back, getting back to the large room with the underground lake. Instead of seeing the moon through the hole in the ceiling, we could now see the sun's light. The sound of the birds came to my ears, and I smiled, knowing that the normal order of things had been restored.

A thought filled my mind, and I turned to Jasper in panic.

"The sun is out! Will you be all right?"

He chuckled. "Do you really think vampires die in the sunlight?"

I froze at his words. "You don't?"

He smiled at me, and I realized this was the first time I was seeing him in daylight. His eyes were deep brown. His skin was paler than mine but still had a little bit of color to it. His brown hair came up to his shoulders. He was truly handsome, and I only fell in love with him more.

"I don't die in the sunlight. But I do appreciate the concern."

He smirked at me, his fangs slightly showing as he winked. A sense of relief overcame me as I realized he wouldn't turn into dust in the sunlight. He cupped my face with his hand, staring at my eyes, his lips brushing against mine as he whispered, "Wow, you're even more beautiful now that the sun is out."

He stole my breath away, sealing his lips on mine, making my heart hammer in my chest. He held me close and asked, "Where shall we go next? We have all eternity to be together."

I could see my soul reflected in his eyes. We were bonded together. I knew I could never live without him.

I started, "Well, I need to get back to my pack and report to them."

He smiled at me. "Fine. Let's take the quickest route."

I wasn't sure what he meant. He grinned as he took me in his arm, holding me tightly. I screamed as our feet left the ground. I grabbed onto Jasper, afraid of falling to the ground. He gave me a loving look.

"Don't worry, love. I won't let you fall."

We flew over the forest. It was beautiful to see nature; finally awaken; after days of darkness. I pointed to the ground as we passed a field of sunflowers.

"Do you like those?" Jasper asked.

"Yes!" I replied, excited. "Those are my favorites."

He smiled. "I think I should call you my little sunflower, then. It suits you well."

I blushed. "You're the second one to call me that."

He chuckled. "The flower that follows the sunlight. A flower of adoration, loyalty, good fortune, and provision."

I smiled at his words. I had never thought of it like that. I liked the fact that he thought of me this way.

"Does this mean you adore me?"

He smiled and tightened his hold on me, landing a kiss on top of my head as we flew.

"Even more than you think."

His words were sincere, and I cuddled even more in his arms, surrounded by his love.

As we landed on my pack's territory, Charles and the other guards came toward us; warily. Werewolves and vampires didn't do well together. Charles's wolf was growling angrily at Jasper.

"Serena, there you are!" shouted Charles.

He tried to grab me, but Jasper kept me in his arms protectively. Charles saw this as an offense and tried to attack Jasper, but I stopped him.

"Charles, stop. He's my mate."

His jaw dropped at those words.

"What the hell? I've never heard of a vampire mate."

I answered gently, "Neither did I, but it's true."

A growl escaped Charles's chest.

"Vampires can't be trusted."

Jasper put his arm protectively around me at those words.

"I know Jasper can be trusted. Please, Charles. We must speak with Alpha David."

Charles stared into my eyes for a moment before nodding reluctantly. "I guess it has something to do with the fact the sun is back."

I nodded to him.

He added angrily, pointing at Jasper.

"You should have waited for us! We're a pack! I'm sure this is all his doing!"

Jasper tensed at Charles's words. I squeezed his arm, pushing through his mind, *"Let me deal with him."*

I felt Jasper's body relax at those words.

I hissed at Charles, "How dare you say something like that? You weren't there. You don't know what happened. Don't be quick to judge on appearances or race. I wouldn't have thought you were like that, Charles. I thought you were my friend."

Guilt spread on Charles's face. Had I been too harsh? He was still a friend, and I didn't want to hurt him, but I needed him to respect my mate.

He muttered, "Sorry."

He didn't say anything more and let us go to the Alpha.

Esme was with David when we entered the room. They were talking with Matthew, Elisen, Kelly, and Theo. They turned toward us.

"You did it!" said Matthew, smiling.

"Serena! Finally! You're back!" shouted Molly happily. The little girl ran into my arms and gave me a big hug. I tickled and kissed her back before letting her return to her parents.

David was smiling, and Esme came and hugged me. David kept his distance. Everyone was staring at Jasper.

"Who is your friend here?" David asked.

Jasper bowed his head slightly to the Alpha.

"This is Jasper. He is my mate."

Esme smiled at my words. David's eyes widened.

"I didn't know it worked with vampires, too."

Jasper smiled. "Neither did I."

Everyone was looking at Jasper, studying him. We had never had a vampire in the pack's house before. David studied him for a moment.

"I love Serena like my own child, Jasper. If you are truly her mate, please love her with all your soul, and care for her. Then I will believe that some vampires can be good."

Jasper put his arms around me lovingly.

"I will do whatever it takes for you to believe it."

David smiled at those words and relaxed, along with everyone else in the room. As the Alpha of my pack, it was important that he approved of my mate. It was anchored at the core of my beliefs since I was raised with werewolves, even if I didn't have a wolf myself.

I told everyone about everything that had happened: how Hemera was kept prisoner by Nyx and Erebus, how we tried to go back to warn the pack but were caught. How we fought together to free the Goddess of the Day, and how she took care of Nyx and Erebus, taking them back to the Underworld.

"You did well, my child," said Esme.

I smiled at her, and then I listened to Matthew's story. I was devastated to learn that Gregory was the necromancer. I understood then how the relic had been stolen, as he had seen and heard me when I had hidden it. But none of it mattered now, as it was over.

"It's almost time for our pack to leave," added David.

Matthew looked happier than ever. I looked at them all and asked, "Can… Can Jasper come with us?"

David sighed at my question, staring at Jasper.

"I know he's your mate." He turned toward Jasper. "No offense. You have my thanks for what you did to free the Goddess of the Day. But some of our members wouldn't be able to accept a vampire among our ranks."

My heart broke at his words. Tears started to flow down my cheeks.

I pleaded, "Please, Alpha. Jasper is my fated mate. Decided by the Moon Goddess."

Esme squeezed my hands in hers, speaking softly, "Even so, people take years to change their minds. This is too sudden.

And just as we're moving away. It is too much for them to accept this."

My legs fell from under me, and I fell to the ground. After everything we went through, I couldn't believe they were asking me to leave Jasper. Our souls were woven together. He was mine, and I was his.

Jasper's strong arms picked me up from the ground.

He whispered softly while wiping off my tears, "Hey, my little sunflower. Don't cry. There's no way I can live without you. Why don't you move with me to the vampire's castle?"

I looked up at him.

"Do you think they'll accept me?"

He nodded. "I am a precious guard to the Vampire Lord. The one he chose to restore daylight when the sun did not rise. He will grant me that favor, I am sure. We'll make it work."

David smiled. "I can see you are a good man, Jasper. Please take good care of her. Maybe one day, our people will understand each other and be able to live together."

Jasper answered, "Of course! I would give my life for her."

Esme asked, worry filling her voice, "Are you sure? Our pack is leaving soon. You won't be able to come back if you change your mind."

I stared into Jasper's eyes. They were full of love and hope. In them, I could see myself and my future. I knew he would always be there for me.

"I am."

I said farewell to everyone. Matthew hugged me and looked at me proudly, "I know that great things will come for you, my dear friend."

I looked at him, then at Elisen and Molly. I was happy the pack was moving so he would be saved. He will make a great Alpha when the time comes.

"The same for you, Matthew," I answered back.

He smiled warmly and hugged me firmly.

Molly came running. I grabbed her in my arms and gave her the biggest hug possible. She landed a wet kiss on my cheek.

"I will miss you, Serena."

I caressed her hair. "We'll see each other again, I promise."

I let the little girl return to her parents and waved at everyone. Jasper lifted me from the ground, a grin on his face. He kissed me lovingly, our tongues dancing together, our hearts beating together. Through our bond, I could feel how happy he was that I chose to go with him. In his arms, I thought of everything that awaited me; the time we'll spend together, the nights filled with pleasure, and maybe even a family. I couldn't wait to live with him forever.

Matthew's POV

*** A few days later ***

I had never thought this day would come. Our pack was finally moving away. It was happening, and it meant one thing to me; I wouldn't need to be sacrificed, and I was given a chance to live.

I grabbed my little girl in my arms and squeezed Elisen's hand lovingly as I started walking. Behind me, I was leaving a life filled mostly with sadness and the fear of being sacrificed. We were also leaving behind DeMörder's followers, who were allowed to live peacefully together. I was against it, but my father was a kind Alpha who believed in second chances. All of it didn't matter now.

In front of us were Odilia and Garry. They walked hand in hand, and I felt happy for their love. Odilia had been through so much, and they both deserved happiness. Molly loved them like an aunt and an uncle, so I would ensure we stayed close.

I was eager to start a new life with my mate. We could even have a child of our own. Molly would always stay my daughter, but I would love to see what happens when a soul nymph and a werewolf have a baby together.

"I can't wait to find out either," whispered Elisen lovingly.

Kelly was walking with Theo by my side. She asked, "To find out what?"

I turned to her. "If I can add another pup to my family."

Kelly giggled. "Well, you're going to meet ours first."

Elisen gasped. "Are you pregnant?"

Elisen shrieked when Kelly nodded. I patted Theo on the back. "Congratulations," I said as Kelly and Elisen talked lively.

"What's happening?" asked Molly in my arms.

I smiled at her. "You're going to have a new baby cousin."

A feeling of peace filled me as we walked toward our new future.

Epilogue (Ravynne)

The attack

*** Centuries later, about thirty years before the events of A Beloved Sin ***

I cast another spell, a bolt of ice piercing the orc's heart. The screech from the creature penetrated the air. I panted and wiped the sweat from my forehead as I watched him fall to the ground. Finally, the last one was dead! I don't know if I would have been able to last much longer.

Around me was destruction. Dead bodies everywhere. The members of our pack mixed with the orcs. No one knew where they came from, but a scary thought crept into my mind. The sin our pack had committed was coming back to haunt us. We were the Goddess's wards, and even though we ran away from this curse centuries ago, it was catching up to us.

I swallowed back the bile that rose to my mouth. My heart hurt from the breaking of the mate bond. He had died on the battlefield with everyone else. I thanked the Goddess that I wasn't born with a wolf, as the bond is harder to break when one of the mates is a wolf. Luckily, I was only a spell caster, but it still hurt like nothing I had ever felt.

I returned to the pack's house, where the children and teenagers were hiding.

"Mom!" shouted my daughter as I entered.

Her deep brown eyes stared at me. As she grew older, she became even more beautiful, looking more like her father with her tawny skin. I knew one day she'd find her mate. My sweet Jasmine, almost an adult now, my precious treasure. I would protect her against our pack's curse. She will not fall to the Goddess's gift.

She asked worryingly, "Where's Dad?"

A knot formed in my stomach. How was I to announce this to my daughter? Everyone's eyes were on me. They were all waiting for news of their parents. My heart broke as I knew what I needed to say would shatter their souls.

"The orcs are dead, but… I'm sorry. Everyone else perished in battle."

The room filled with tears and cries. But we were a pack, a family. Broken, they held each other in their arms, comforting each other as a pack should.

My daughter asked me, "What are we going to do?"

I spoke strongly, looking at everyone.

"Together, we will rebuild, stand our ground, and stand again as a pack. It will take time, but I know we can work together."

They nodded at me, too broken to cheer, but I could see a glimpse of hope in their eyes. It would take years for our wounds to heal, and much work awaited us. But I knew we could do it together.

Today, I became the Alpha of the pack. We would build a new pack, standing strong against the Goddess's curse. For I swear, there will never be another sacrifice.

A word from the author

Hi,

I really hope you enjoyed The Goddess's Wards. Please don't forget to leave a review on Amazon and Goodreads. Reviews are the best way to support authors.

The first book of my series, Age-Old Enemies, has been scripted and presented to producers. You should check out the series so you can compare when a movie is made.

https://www.amazon.com/gp/product/B09DB1TVC6

If you've never read A Beloved Sin before, then you should check it out. It's the second book of the Mate Longing series (after Age-Old Enemies). You will see what happens to Ravynne and the pack of werewolf-witches. It's available in French and English on Amazon.

https://www.amazon.com/dp/B09S4THG9Z

My next series, Blood and Kisses, is coming soon. Fate has a wicked plan for a young prince, born from the love of a werewolf and a vampire. The world will have changed a lot when this young prince becomes a king… He will be the main character of the next series. You can already add Book 1 – Cursed King, to your "Want to read" list on Goodreads.

https://www.goodreads.com/book/show/105735229-cursed-king

Finally, you might want to check out what happens to Molly, the adoptive daughter of Matthew and Elisen, in an all new series called Half-angel's daughter. Book 1 will be called – Devoured by Darkness, and you can already add it to your "Want to read" list on Goodreads.

https://www.goodreads.com/book/show/111371393-devoured-by-darkness

Don't forget to subscribe to my mailing list! And if you feel like it, go on my website, and drop me an email. I'd love to learn more about you! What do you like? What's your favorite trope? What do you despise?

Thank you for your love and support,

Danielle Paquette-Harvey

daniellephauthor.com

Acknowledgments

I want to thank all my amazing readers. A story without readers has no purpose, and so, I wouldn't be able to do it without you. This story came to life because of you. You all loved A Beloved Sin so much, that you asked for more. You wanted to know where Leila's pack came from, and what happened to them, and so I gave it to you. I sincerely hope that you loved it. Your reviews and comments are the fire that keeps me burning!

I want to thank my husband, Martin, and my kids. Once again, thank you for being patient with me as I spend hours writing and editing. Thank you for listening to all my book talk and ideas. I know I always talk about books all the time, but thank you for listening. I love you from the bottom of my heart!

My soul triplets. Where would I be without you? You guys allow me to go through my darkest hours and I feel alone without you. I can't wait for us three to meet in person and laugh, drink, and be crazy together.

I also want to thank all my friends. Your love and affection is what keeps me going. Whether I know you virtually or in person, So many people write to me every day, and I can't always answer to everyone properly, but know that I'm truly grateful for your friendship and support.

Love you guys! See you soon.

Danielle

Check out the rest of my work. All my books are available on Amazon. Some of them are also available in Barn & Nobels stores and other libraries across the world.

Prequel to the Longing mates series
- The prophecy - ISBN 978-1777572105

Longing mates Series

A powerful, alluring vampire prince. The strong daughter of the Alpha. Born enemies, tied by an unbreakable bond. Multiple times Best Seller in different countries. Read the series that started it all.

1. Age-Old Enemies - ISBN 978-1777572136
2. A Beloved Sin - ISBN 978-1777572150
3. The Fallen - ISBN 978-1-7782178-5-2

Blood and Kisses Series
2. Cursed King – coming soon

Half-angel's daughter Series
2. Devoured by Darkness – coming soon

Charity books

- A Wicked Taste of Fate – An Anthology - ISBN 978-1-7782178-6-9